Mike Faricy

Crickett

Published by

Credit River Publishing 2015

Copyright Mike Faricy 2014

Crickett

ISBN 13: 978-1507506370

ISBN 10: 1507506376

Acknowledgments

I would like to thank the following people for their help and support:

Special thanks to Kitty, Donna, Rhonda for their hard work, cheerful patience and positive feedback.

I would like to thank Dan, Julie, Sam & Roy for their creative talent and not slitting their wrists or jumping off the high bridge when dealing with my Neanderthal computer capabilities.

Last, I would like to thank family and friends for their encouragement and unqualified support. Special thanks to Maggie, Jed, Schatz, Pat, Emily, Pat and Av for not rolling their eyes, at least when I was there, and most of all, to my wife Teresa whose belief, support and inspiration has from day one never waned.

To Teresa

"God, you idjit!"

Crickett

<u>Chapter One</u>

I dropped into The Spot for only one, four hours ago. Just as I signaled Mike for another, I caught sight of her walking in the side door. Karen Riley hadn't changed much in a year and a half. She did seem to bounce a little more enticingly as she came around the bar, of course that was before I saw the stroller with the baby. Two serious drinkers at the end of the bar had to move their stools so she could get past and they didn't look too happy about the interruption.

On our last night out she was staggering after drinking two bottles of pink champagne, she slipped getting into my car. As her skirt rose up around her waist she looked over her shoulder at me, licked her lips then said, "Maybe you'd like to give a girl a hand?"

I was only too willing to lend a helping grope.

Amazingly, the ride home had been uneventful, but only because I was able to fend Karen off despite her protestations. Before we'd driven a block she'd slipped her skirt off and tossed it onto the spare tire in the back seat. More than once I had to physically keep her at bay as we raced toward her house.

"Just pull over and let's do it, Dev. Come on," she sighed then ripped her blouse open.

We were only four minutes away from her place. I figured I could hang on, but sped up all the same. She seemed to settle down as I screeched around the corner onto her street. I pulled to the curb in front of her place, jumped out then quickly walked around to open her door.

It had all the makings of a night to remember and I rubbed my hands in delicious anticipation. As I opened the passenger door her purse fell to the ground, followed by her gorgeous legs swinging invitingly onto the sidewalk in a very unlady-like pose. She looked up at me with a glassy stare, but I don't think she saw me. Fortunately, at a little after three in the morning no one would be around to notice her thong attire. I stuffed a handful of items back into her purse then picked up a discarded red heel from the curb. Halfway along her stagger toward the front door she kicked the other shoe into the garden. She let her blouse fall to the ground just before the front steps. I stopped to retrieve it juggling her purse and the heels.

"It's been real, later baby," she slurred just as I heard the front door click open and she staggered inside. I clutched everything in my arms and hurried up the porch steps. I had five feet to go when she slammed the door closed behind her, stumbled into the middle of the living room then passed out on the floor.

I could see her through the front window, lying face down on the carpeted floor, wearing just her thong and a gold necklace, out cold. I rang the doorbell repeatedly. I pounded on the locked door then frantically searched around the porch for a nonexistent key. She remained dead to the world.

A clap of thunder brought me to my senses. I carried her shoes, purse and blouse back to my car. I tossed them on top of her skirt and the spare tire just as the rain began to pour down.

I don't know, maybe it was karma, bad karma I guess. I was back over there the following afternoon shampooing her living room rug and not having much luck removing the pink champagne stain.

Pasty looking Karen didn't seem to be in the best of moods stretched out on her living room couch. A blue terricloth robe was cinched tightly around her waist hiding any semblance of her figure and eliminating my hope of a 'thank you'. She had an ice pack on her head, a box of Kleenex on her lap and occasionally sipped from a glass of 7-Up. When she spoke it was only to give me further rug cleaning directions or swear that she would never, ever drink pink champagne again.

I came back to reality as she forced the stroller around a table, flashed a smile in my direction then charged toward me pushing a wide-eyed little boy. The words 'Paternity Suit' suddenly screamed in my head. I wasn't sure if it was the stroller with all the toys or the gigantic diaper bag that made her look like she was getting ready to set up a campsite.

"Well, well, well, Dev Haskell. I thought I might find you here," she said then proceeded to hoist the diaper bag onto the bar.

I had to clear my throat a couple of times before I could find my voice. "Great to see you again, Karen," I lied. "Who is this little guy?" I asked then gripped the edge of the bar and waited for the shotgun blast.

"This is our little Oliver, ten months. Oh, and just so you know, I've changed my name. Now I'm Crickett."

7

I felt light headed as the color drained from my face. I was too stunned to do the math in my head, nine months plus ten months before that equals when?

"Oh, Jesus, Dev calm down. God, look at you, you're pale as a ghost. Are you gonna be okay? It's Daryl and me, he's my boyfriend."

I still wasn't seeing anything funny in my honest mistake, but I faked it. "Well congratulations, Kar... I mean, Crickett. And aren't you the handsome little devil," I said looking down, actually he kind of was. I felt my heart slowing back down to normal. "What's with the Crickett name change?"

"Oh, Karen was just, I don't know, so proper, so churchy. Crickett is more me, more of my persona."

'Persona,' I thought. "Can I get you something?"

Mike strolled up and studied her from across the bar.

"Gee, thanks, but I better not. Course on second thought, maybe just a double Bombay Sapphire martini and two olives," she said all the while staring at Oliver. She shrugged her shoulders, shook her head back and forth and made a strange face at the baby.

"You want a bag of beer nuts or maybe some pork rinds for the little guy?" I asked.

"Ahhh, no I don't think so and his name's Oliver, Dev. If he gets hungry I'll just feed him. Yes, Oliver you're growing up to be a great big boy, aren't you? Yes, yes mommy's little moose." She sort of squeaked out the word 'moose' and the serious drinkers who'd had to move their stools glanced down the bar.

We chatted for a bit. At least I tried to chat. Crickett was busy making faces at Oliver and sipping her martini. She drained the glass, pushed it across the bar signaling for another, then turned toward me and thrust her chest out to take control of the conversation.

"Daryl and I need your help. It's kind of embarrassing, but I figured you're used to it."

"Being embarrassed?"

She nodded then said, "Yeah, you know the sort of situations you seem to get yourself into. Remember when you had that crazy woman who tried to kill you?"

"Which one, there've been more than a couple?"

She nodded like that sounded perfectly logical. "Well, of course I'd like to hear their side. Thanks," she said to Mike as he slid another filled to the rim martini in front of her.

"So what happened?"

She took a deep breath, a healthy sip then said, "Daryl was arrested, and our attorney said he should try to make a deal, only he didn't do anything."

I nodded like this made sense. Actually, in my line of work it sort of did.

Crickett looked around, then leaned forward and half whispered. "He was arrested with some drugs in his possession. Only he didn't know they were in his possession."

"Did someone plant them on him?"

"Sort of."

"How much are we talking about?"

"They said five million, at least that's the figure from the DEA, but I'm thinking they trumped it up. You know how they are."

"Even so, five million? That's not exactly an amount you can hide in your jacket pocket."

Oliver began to fuss at this point, and I half wondered if he somehow understood the gravity of his father's situation.

"Oh God, he can't be hungry. I'll tell you, all he does is eat," Crickett said. She didn't look all that thrilled as she lifted Oliver out of his stroller and onto her lap. Even I had to admit, for ten months he was a pretty big guy.

"Do you want to grab that booth in the back so you can have little more privacy?"

"Oh honestly, it's completely natural, Dev, it's why God gave them to us," she said then pulled her top up, exposed her left breast and flashed a smile in my direction. It looked a lot larger than I remembered, and I stared while she took another healthy sip of her martini. Little Oliver clamped on the moment she set her glass down. Once attached, he turned his head and gave me a look as if to say, *'See what I got and you can't have any.'* The drinkers at the end of the bar suddenly looked a lot happier, stared for a long moment then ordered another round.

Chapter Two

Crickett went on to explain her boyfriend's predicament while little Oliver remained firmly attached. I suspected, given his male genes that he was just showing off, possession being nine-tenths of the law.

"So that's pretty much it. He just thought he was helping out a friend, driving this van into the parking ramp. They have him on video the entire way."

"The police?"

She nodded. "Yeah, I haven't actually seen the thing. I guess the video is like fifteen minutes long, including his arrest. It's just so obvious it was all a set up."

"Well, yeah, but he was arrested in possession of the van and there was five-million dollars worth of drugs in the thing. I'm guessing you don't hide that much in the glove compartment."

"Apparently they were all stacked up on a pallet in the back. Actually, two pallets I guess, but there was a tarp over them so he didn't really know. Anyway, we're going to dispute the five-million figure. I think it sounds high."

"Jesus. Who owns the van?"

"It was a rental."

"Who rented it?"

"Well, I guess it was supposed to be rented, but actually it was sort of just taken."

"You mean stolen?"

She gave a nonchalant nod then adjusted Oliver who seemed to be contentedly sleeping and still latched to mommy. The little glutton opened his eyes for a brief moment and shot me another glance that suggested *'Don't even think about it.'* Then he snuggled in closer and drifted back asleep.

"Did Daryl steal the van?" I asked.

"Well, that's what the police are saying. It's one of the charges against him. But the keys were under the floor mat so he just got in and drove off."

"And he was going to deliver this van to a parking ramp?"

She nodded like this made perfect sense.

Daryl wasn't sounding like the brightest bulb on the tree. His credibility was becoming an issue with me and I hadn't even met the guy.

"So what about the friend he was helping? Was he arrested too?"

"Not exactly. See, that's sort of the problem or at least one of the problems. We can't seem to find him. No one knows where he is, and then Daryl got this warning not to cooperate with the police." She leaned forward, glanced around cautiously, and whispered. "They said if he cooperated, Oliver and I would be killed."

Little Oliver suddenly began to suck viciously.

"Who's *'they'*?"

"We don't know. I'm guessing the drug people, but I don't have any names."

"The drug people." I wasn't sure where to begin. Every statement seemed to raise a half dozen common sense questions. Not the least of which was *'Could Daryl really be this stupid?'*

"Honestly, Crickett, I'm not sure what I can do here. Do you have a lawyer?"

She nodded. "We have a public defender, but she's really busy. She's the one who told Daryl to make a deal."

"Was she aware of the threat on your life?"

"Yeah, Daryl told her about it, but she said it didn't seem credible."

"Not credible? How would she know? What's her name?"

"Daphne…"

I waited for the bomb to drop, if it was Daphne Cochrane, I knew her as Daft, but had called her less charitable things. A few years back she had briefly been my court appointed public defender. I dropped her the moment she suggested I plead guilty to a murder charge. She was an eternally unhappy, impressed with herself, Ivy League, condescending witch who….

"Cochrane. Daphne Cochrane. She seems very smart."

'Yeah, and she'd be only too happy to tell you how very smart she is,' I thought.

"Do you know her?" Crickett asked.

"Not really," I said and let it go at that.

"I was wondering if maybe you could, you know, do some investigation or something so they drop the charges against Daryl."

"Crickett, did you talk to your lawyer, Daphne about this? Clear it with her?"

"She's sort of busy and well, like I said, she wants Daryl to cooperate with the police and hopefully he can

13

get some kind of deal. You know a reduced sentence and stuff. I just don't know."

I did know and if the threat to harm Crickett and baby Oliver was even halfway credible there was a good chance they would be killed and then once Daryl knew they were dead whoever was behind their murder would have him killed, too.

"I think you should request protection for starters. Tell your lawyer, Daphne that these folks aren't fooling around. If Daryl is going to cooperate, you two have to be safe. These drug folks aren't kidding. That size of a drug bust, five million, you've most likely got some pretty angry bad guys out there right about now. She can't just dismiss your concern. If she does then you should go straight to her boss."

"Yeah. I don't know it all seems so complicated."

"Complicated? Crickett, these are serious charges. He could be looking at twenty years."

"Daphne thought more like twenty-five, but she said he could get out in fifteen with good behavior." She said sounding like that was a really positive development.

"Fifteen years is still a lot, particularly if he's innocent."

"I suppose. But if you did some investigating then you could tell the police he's innocent, they'd let him go, he wouldn't have to cooperate and we would be safe," she said then half pulled little Oliver off the feed bag.

He quickly reattached himself.

"Crickett, I can look into some basics, maybe talk to the police, but your best bet is getting some protection and like I said, if your attorney doesn't want to do that maybe call her boss or ask for someone else to represent you."

"So you won't check? You won't investigate?"

"No, I mean, yes. I'll at least check on some of the basics. But let me be honest, based on what you've told me, this is what's referred to as an open and shut case. Even if we can prove Daryl is innocent…"

"Oh, I guess he most likely is, maybe."

Not the sort of ringing endorsement I would have hoped for. "Well, we still have an uphill fight on our hands, not only to prove he's innocent, but to get the charges against him dropped. And, look I'm willing to help, I'll do some initial checking, but at some point I'll have to charge you and this could get expensive very quickly."

She nodded like it was no big thing then said, "Okay, how soon before you can start your investigation?"

An image flashed across my mind. Crickett lying on her couch in that dreadful blue terri-cloth robe while I worked at mission impossible, attempting to shampoo two bottles worth of pink champagne out of her living-room carpet.

"I'll see if I can interview Daryl tomorrow. Let me get some general information from you first," I said and pulled one of the envelopes out of my back pocket so I could write some notes on the thing.

Chapter Three

"Yeah, and that's not the worst of it. The van was stolen," I said to Louie. He's my attorney. We share an office along with a number of wasted nights and some pretty vicious hangovers.

Louie leaned back in his office chair and put his feet up on the picnic table that served as his desk.

I continued to look through my binoculars into the third-floor apartment across the street hoping to spot one of the women who lived there. I wasn't having much luck.

"The van was stolen?"

"Yeah, like I said it get's worse. His pal told him the keys were under the floor mat. Innocent idiot Daryl Bergstrom drives off in the thing with two pallets of cocaine bricks sitting in the back under a tarp. He drives to a downtown parking ramp and apparently never questions any of this. Crickett said some pal paid him a hundred bucks to leave the van in the parking ramp. The cops have him on tape from the moment he gets in the van until his arrest in the parking ramp. I talked to someone down there and I'll see the tape tomorrow, but they've got this jackass nailed a hundred ways to Sunday."

"And someone is threatening your ex and her baby?"

"Ex is maybe too strong a term, we weren't together long enough to rate that title."

"She dumped you?"

"More like a mutual lack of interest. Although doing the math she must have been seeing this Daryl character at the same time. To tell you the truth, I'm guessing I was the dalliance or maybe a brief interruption and he was the steady boyfriend."

"When are you going to see this guy?"

"Tomorrow, right after I watch the surveillance video of him taking the van and then driving it into the parking ramp."

"It sure sounds like a setup. The cops are there filming, just waiting for someone to show up and drive off in the thing," Louie shook his head in disbelief.

"I'm guessing whoever the pal was with the hundred bucks, he knew what was going down or had some awfully strong suspicions. The cops weren't just filming, apparently they had a tracking device planted on the van, as well. Of course they've also got this numbskull on the parking ramp security cameras. Oh, and one of their undercover officers follows him into the ramp and parks about four spaces away on the same level."

"And he's clueless?"

"Apparently. Yeah, it's a setup, I think there's a good chance my guy is innocent of any drug offense along with guilty of being really stupid. But, that doesn't alter the facts and the facts are not in his favor, at least from what I can see."

Louie shook his head, then drained his glass and pushed it across the picnic table toward me. "After all that, I could use a little more to soothe my nerves."

17

I put the binoculars down on the window sill, poured a good inch into his glass and capped the fifth of Jameson.

"Not having any?"

"I gotta go to some fundraiser tonight with Heidi and be on my best behavior."

"Fundraiser?"

"I don't know, some political thing. Anyway, it usually works in my favor. I'll be her designated driver while she hob knobs with the 'Swells'. Oh, get this, just in case things aren't bad enough for this Daryl dude, guess who's representing him?"

Louie took a sip and shrugged.

"Daft."

"Cochrane? Daphne Cochrane? God, poor bastard doesn't have a snowball's chance in hell. I hope you advised your lady friend to get another lawyer."

"Yeah, I did, but I think it just went in one ear and out the other."

"Mind if I make a suggestion?" Louie said then drained his glass. "He needs to cooperate, give his pal's name to the cops, hell, they probably already know who it is. Then he needs to get away from Daft. She'll get him sentenced to twenty years, killed, or both. I'll represent him pro bono if need be, but get him away from her, she shouldn't even be practicing."

"That's big of you."

"The M.O. fits in with my usual band of idiots. I can use the publicity and it won't cost me anything more than a little of my time."

"I'll pass it on," I said, then picked up the binoculars to resume my futile quest.

Chapter Four

I was seated at Heidi's kitchen counter paging through some dreadfully trashy magazine full of makeup tips and an expose on a Hollywood star I'd never, ever heard of. I'd been sitting there for the past half hour while Heidi tried on a dozen different outfits. All the while she was racing back and forth between her walk-in closet and the full length mirror in her bedroom she called to me. "I'll just be another minute."

"No rush."

"Almost ready," she called five minutes later.

"No problem, take your time."

She carried two different outfits on hangers from the closet then held them in front of her while she stood staring at the large mirror. I could hear her mumbling, "Oh, I don't know."

Truth be told, she looked fabulous in everything she'd tried on. She could have gone to the event in cut-offs and a T-shirt and still have been the most attractive woman there. But, painful past experience had taught me to keep my opinion to myself at this particular moment.

She strolled into the kitchen fifteen minutes later hooking an earring and looking like a million bucks. "What do you think?" she asked.

It's one of those questions like *'Does this dress make my ass look fat?'* or *'How old do you think I am?'* You're juggling a grenade and hoping the pin wouldn't fall out.

"I don't think you should wear that. It makes you look stunningly beautiful and every guy there will be hitting on you. I better go back home and get my gun."

"Stop, you're just saying that."

"Beautiful, Heidi, really nice." I was telling the truth.

"You don't think it's showing too much cleavage? I don't know, maybe I should wear a different bra."

"I think you're asking the wrong guy. I got an idea, let's skip this fundraiser and I'll send them a check for a hundred bucks. We'll stay here, just the two of us, and your wine glass will never be empty."

"Yeah, you'd love it. That's my going rate a measly hundred bucks?"

"Actually, I would love to stay here, and I'm sure my personal check would be acceptable."

"Hmm-mmm, too bad, come on we better get going. We're already late," she said making it sound like I had something to do with the tardy departure.

We made the short drive to downtown St. Paul and I pulled into the valet parking lane. I figured parking would probably run me twenty bucks, and we weren't even inside. The eighteen-year-old valet opened the passenger door for Heidi, then stood and stared at her with a ravenous look on his baby face. Apparently he agreed with me. He came to his senses after a long moment and walked over to me. "Man, I don't believe it, just like Walter White," he said as I handed him the keys to my Pontiac Aztek.

"It's been giving me a little trouble lately," I said failing to mention it had been a pain for the past ten months. He was still trying to start it when we walked into the reception area.

"Well, Heidi. My, my, aren't we looking grand," some guy said then planted a lingering kiss on her check. "Here, will a white do?" he asked and handed her one of the two glasses of wine he was carrying.

"Burt, how sweet," she cooed. "Say, I'd like you to meet a friend of mine, Dev Haskell. Dev, meet Burt," Heidi giggled.

Burt nodded and extended his hand. As we shook, he sort of half turned and cut me off. "Heidi, I wonder if I could have a private momentito. If you'd excuse us for just a bit, Dan," he said over his shoulder then hurried her off to a corner explaining some sort of involved thing I apparently wouldn't be able to comprehend.

I made my way to the bar, got a lite beer in a bottle for eight dollars and began to mingle. The fundraiser had a bar set up in all four corners of the large, chandeliered ballroom. None of them offered a decent beer, but then these were 'The Swells' and I was out of my usual drinking element. I figured there might be a good three hundred plus people milling around paying exorbitant drink prices and trying to look interesting. I recognized a few people, but no one I really wanted to talk to. I couldn't see Heidi anywhere, but a casual glance around confirmed she would be the most attractive woman in attendance.

I finished my lousy beer and got another. I caught Heidi from across the room involved in an animated conversation with two guys, neither one Burt. I decided to stay away and wandered over to the hors d'oeuvres table. I could have saved the effort.

Apparently this was some sort of gluten free, vegan group. Not so much as a Dorito, cocktail wiener, or a meatball to save my soul. Most of the food trays were already picked over and empty, but the signs were still sitting on the table in front of the crumb-covered trays; Broccoli au Grande, Cauliflower Au lait, persimmon, avocado cubes. I could go on, but you catch my drift. I would have killed for a double cheeseburger or a Ballpark hot dog.

I was ready to leave anytime, but this was actually business for Heidi. She would be talking to clients or prospective clients all night long. I'd known that was the drill before we arrived. I also knew how she intended to unwind once we got home, so I just sipped the lousy beer and bided my time.

I spotted my target maybe twenty minutes later. In a room full of elegantly tailored outfits, summer silk blouses, delicate lace and sprayed on tans there she was in a gray wool skirt, with a red sweater draped over her shoulders. It looked like the perfect winter outfit for an elementary school principal. Unfortunately, it was July in Minnesota with an evening temp still hovering close to ninety and a dew point not far behind. Daft, Daphne Cochrane, Daryl Bergstrom's appointed public defender, small world.

She appeared adrift in an endless sea of chatty, head-bobbing individuals waxing eloquently about nothing while they stood in small groups all around her. She lifted a wine glass to her lips, but at just about the point where the wine approached the rim, she lowered the glass.

She appeared to be alone. Over the course of the four or five minutes I watched, she spoke to no one and no one spoke to her. If she was waiting for a friend, they were sure taking their sweet time. Not to sound too cruel, but it seemed obvious her reputation had preceded her or maybe it was just the cat hair on her sweater.

I approached with caution.

"Excuse me. Are you Ms Cochrane with the public defenders office?"

She studied me for a moment, but didn't seem to recognize me as yet another disappointed and poorly-served former client. Finally she nodded.

"I've seen you in the courtroom. How are you doing?"

"Just fine, thank you," she said crisply, but gave no follow-up question like asking my name, wondering if I practiced law, maybe sat on the bench, or was just another criminal.

"I understand you're involved in this most recent case, the one where the fellow drove the van loaded with drugs over to the parking ramp?"

She gave a slight nod and took a fake sip.

"What was his name, David something?"

"Actually, Daryl, Daryl Bergstrom."

"How is that going, do you have a trial date assigned yet?"

"No, I'm hoping we can work out a plea agreement and avoid any sort of a trial."

She'd already told me more than she should have. Based on what I'd observed, it couldn't be the wine talking, she hadn't had any. I chalked it up to ineptness.

"How does your client feel about that?"

She sighed and said, "Well, actually at this point, let's just say we're still in the initial discussion stage." She flashed a quick, cold smile. Obviously, if her innocent clients were locked up, she wouldn't have to waste her time in the court room.

"Always a pleasure chatting with you, Ms. Cochrane."

She gave a slight nod like this was an excepted fact then looked at me dismissively so I nodded and drifted back into the crowd.

Louie was right, and all my initial fears had just been confirmed, Daryl Bergstrom was royally screwed. I paid ten bucks for a glass of lousy white wine and located Heidi. She was surrounded by four paunchy guys vying for her attention. She looked grateful to see me.

"Oh, here is my significant other, Dev come here and join us. Oh, thanks," she said taking the glass of wine and handing me her empty. She took two very healthy gulps and smiled.

Two of the guys nodded and quickly left, a third stayed a half moment longer before he fled to the bar. The fourth guy hung in there for maybe five minutes talking some investment scheme that even I thought sounded shady. When he left, Heidi smiled sweetly, looked around, and said "Thanks for the rescue. He wanted to take me up to his cabin tonight."

"Can't blame him for trying. I'm ready whenever you are."

"Maybe just a while longer, I'm picking up some business."

"Like at that guy's cabin?"

"Oh, be nice. Maybe once I finish this glass of wine we'll go somewhere a little more private."

<u>Chapter Five</u>

It was a little after ten the following morning
when my phone rang. By the time I stumbled out of bed
and found my trousers in Heidi's living room, whoever
it was had hung up. Against my better judgment I
pulled the phone out of the pocket and called back.

"Hello." I recognized Crickett's pleading voice
immediately and flashed awake.

"Crickett, its Dev Haskell. You just called me."

"Oh, Dev, God, Daryl's dead."

"What?"

"I got the call about an hour ago. Someone killed
him in jail."

"Killed him? In the jail?

"That's what they said. I've been sitting here not
knowing what to do so I thought I'd call you."

I could hear Oliver in the background.

"Oh, not this again," Crickett said.

"Give me your address and I'll come over."

"Is that okay? I'm sorry, I'm just sort of at a loss.
I'm not sure what to do and, alright I'm coming, I'm
coming. Sorry, I better go."

"You still in the same place?"

What? Oh no, we, I guess I should say just me, now. I have a different place.

"Give me the address, Crickett."

"Oh yeah, I 'spose."

I kept repeating Crickett's address until I found a pencil and wrote it down. Actually it was some sort of eyebrow makeup pencil thing I found on Heidi's kitchen counter. It had been lying next to the blender. I'd made a couple of batches of Pina Coladas last night when we finally got home. There was maybe half a glass left in the blender, but I thought I'd better give it a pass.

Heidi was sound asleep and I didn't want to wake her, she'd certainly earned it. I showered, dressed, put the coffee on for her and left a note. I pulled up in front of Crickett's less than fifteen minutes later.

Her new place was a nice two-story structure with a brick and timber second floor, wood shutters on both sides of all the windows, and three steep peaks on the roof. A brick walk curved in a gentle 'S' pattern across the groomed front lawn and up to the front door. Nice digs for a 'single' mom whose boyfriend was locked up and looking at twenty to twenty-five years. I climbed the buff stone steps and pushed the doorbell, it chimed from somewhere inside.

Crickett opened the door a moment after the chimes stopped. "Hi, Dev, gee thanks for coming right over. I hope I didn't interrupt anything."

I had expected red puffy eyes, mascara running down her cheeks, and a fist full of Kleenex. To tell the truth she looked pretty well put together. Nicely put together as a matter of fact.

"Crickett, I just want to say how sorry I am. Actually, I sort of don't know what to say. This is all so, I don't know, not just unexpected, it's shocking."

"Yeah, I guess so."

"What did they say? The police just called? They didn't send someone over to inform you personally?"

"The cops? Oh no, they didn't call. I got the call from Daryl's father, Charlie. Apparently someone went to his house this morning, he lives out of town. I was only on the phone with him for a minute or two. We don't really get along, he's kind of a pain in the ass, if you know what I mean?" She shrugged, then said, "Actually, there s no 'kind of' about it, he's a pain, a major pain."

"Did he give you any idea what happened?"

"No, but then again he wouldn't. Anyway, I'm supposed to meet him, Charlie, at the morgue at one."

"You okay?" I asked.

"Me? Yeah, in a way I guess it kind of puts a stop to any long, drawn out legal process with a trial, and it certainly makes me and Oliver a lot safer."

I must have given her some sort of look because she quickly added. "I mean, think about it. Now, since Daryl obviously can't cooperate with the police and make some dopey deal, there really isn't much point in someone threatening or harming Oliver and me. Is there?"

"Did you hear from your attorney?"

"No, not a word."

Somehow that didn't seem surprising. I didn't see any point in mentioning I saw Daphne Cochrane last night.

"Want something to drink? Come on back to the kitchen."

I followed her across a nicely furnished living room with a large, heavy, oak staircase climbing up the far wall. We passed what looked like an office/den with a fireplace, walked across a fairly good-sized paneled

27

dining room, then through a swinging door with a brass push plate that led into a spacious kitchen.

There were lots of cabinets and they looked like they were cherry wood. The counter tops were some sort of polished, white marble with gleaming, white subway tiles running up the wall from the counter tops to the upper cabinets. A bag of pancake mix and an empty package of sausage sat abandoned on the counter and a dusting of pancake mix left a trail leading to the gas range. A white, Styrofoam container for a dozen eggs sat open on the far side of the sink and held three eggs. The large kitchen sink held what looked like two crystal champagne flutes, two breakfast plates slick with syrup, and a couple of coffee mugs. Whoever had been here had one hell of an appetite.

Crickett picked up a glass of white wine from the counter. The glass was maybe half full and had condensation along the outside. "You want some wine?"

"Thanks, but I better not. Got any coffee?"

"Yeah, I think there's some left." She opened a cabinet and pulled down a coffee mug that matched the two in the sink. "Cream or sugar?" she asked reaching for a pot that held maybe a half cup.

"Black is just fine."

"Would you like something to eat? I guess since it's almost noon I could call somewhere, maybe get a sandwich delivered or something."

"No thanks, coffee will do."

We chatted for a few minutes until Oliver's screech erupted from some sort of monitor plugged into an outlet. Apparently he was waking up from a nap. "Oh, God, I better go get him or he'll just keep screaming. I've got someone coming over to watch him when I go to the morgue. I'm really not looking forward to that," she said and shot me a glance.

I nodded. I had been to the morgue once or twice before and I knew from past experience it wasn't the first place to go for a fun time.

"Say, Dev," she said and drained her wine glass. "I was just wondering. Could I impose on you to go with me? Daryl's dad can be such a jerk and well, I could really use some moral support."

"The morgue?"

She nodded like it was just an offer to accompany her to the grocery store or a walk around the block. Oliver screeched out from the monitor again.

"God, alright I coming," she said, then jumped up and pushed back through the swinging door mumbling. "Calm down, Jesus I'm coming." She must have been climbing the stairs because her voice gradually faded, a moment later I heard her footsteps overhead while I sat there thinking *the morgue!*

Chapter Six

I'd been here before, and just like before, by the time I caught site of the entrance to the small parking lot, I'd already driven past and had to go around the block. Crickett gave me a quick look, rolled her eyes, but didn't say anything.

As I pulled into the lot she said, "Oh shit, there's Charlie just getting out of his truck. See it, the red pickup?"

There were just five parking spaces so he was pretty hard to miss. He'd grabbed the only spot labeled *'Family Parking'*. I pulled into the spot reserved for police vehicles.

Officially the morgue was called the Ramsey County Medical Examiner's Office. It's a nondescript, one-story tan-brick building, dwarfed by the massive Regions Hospital complex next door. Those of us still breathing entered through the front door emblazoned with an *'Hours 8-4'* sign. The dead were unceremoniously hauled in via the loading dock in back. I wasn't sure what the hours were back there.

"If you open up the glove compartment there's a manila envelope in there. Would you give it to me?"

Crickett opened the glove compartment and handed the envelope to me. I had printed off a *'Police Vehicle Official Business'* sign some time back. I pulled it out of the envelope and placed it on my dashboard. "Let's go."

She waited until Charlie entered the building. She dawdled long enough getting out of my car that it had stopped sputtering by the time she closed her door. We walked in the building and came face to face with Charlie in the small lobby. He was dressed in jeans and a denim work shirt with the sleeves rolled up. He wore a black baseball cap with the words *'Vietnam Veteran'* embroidered across the front.

"Charlie," Crickett said and gave a slight nod.

He nodded back, then glanced at me and muttered, "Figures, I knew it wouldn't take you too long."

"This is Dev Haskell, Charlie. Actually, he's a private eye, he was going to get all the charges dismissed against Daryl, but well…" her voice trailed off, she gave a shrug and then headed for one of the chairs.

"Please accept my condolences, Mr. Bergstrom," I said and held out my hand.

He shook my hand, nodded and sort of gave a sigh like it had already been a very long day. Under the circumstances I could understand.

The lobby was painted a nondescript off-white color with gray carpet. Three framed landscape prints hung on the walls. The ink on the prints had faded over time and gave off an overall bluish cast. A couple of well-tended potted plants sat against an exterior wall growing up toward a small skylight.

An office and file room were just visible behind a thick, tinted glass window that had a round speaking screen set into it. A handwritten note was taped to the glass, *'Ring bell for service.'* Charlie rang the chrome bell, and then said to a shadowy figure on the other side of the tinted glass, "I'm Daryl Bergstrom's father."

A moment later a woman opened a door labeled *'Authorized Personnel Only'* and said, "This way."

She led us to Family Room 101 where we waited in silence for another five minutes. When the door opened again, the same woman said, "If you'd like to come this way, please."

We walked down a short hallway and into a viewing room. The room was small with an industrial gray tile floor. It was devoid of furniture and anything on the walls, but then there really wasn't a need. We approached a curtained window and stood there for what felt like a year until the curtain was drawn back. Daryl Bergstrom was laid out on the other side of the window, draped in a shroud pulled up to his chin. Just his face was visible. He had been cleaned up and looked peaceful if you could see past the battered face. An attendant in a white lab coat stood off to the side.

Crickett let off an audible gasp. Charlie gave an agonized sigh then looked at the woman who had escorted us into the room and nodded. She waited a few moments longer then held the door open for us as we got ready to exit the room.

"If you would come with me, we can get the paper work in order for release," she said.

We filed out of the viewing room with Crickett in the lead making tracks toward the lobby. "You're not gonna need me, are you Charlie?" Crickett said over her shoulder. Her voice seemed to pull him back to the here and now. "I mean you can deal with this, can't you? I hate paperwork and forms and shit." She kept moving toward the lobby door then turned and glanced back at the woman with the surprised look on her face. "We'll barely have time to grab some lunch before I have to get back to the baby."

"I'll handle this," Charlie replied softly.

"Come on, Dev, let's go," Crickett said and opened the door to the lobby.

"I'm terribly sorry, Mr. Bergstrom," I said and held out my hand.

Charlie shook it. He looked like he was still dazed.

"You gonna be okay?" I asked.

"Dev?" Crickett called from the lobby.

Charlie nodded, "Yeah, just want to get this over with. Thanks, like I said, I'll handle it."

"Dev?" Crickett called again.

Chapter Seven

"Fine, you don't want to grab lunch, I guess you can just drop me back at home," Crickett said making it sound like dropping her at home would be a really bad decision on my part. We were sitting at a stoplight in the middle of downtown. I couldn't decide if I should lecture her on basic civility, or just kick her out of my car and make her walk the rest of the way. The light changed and the Aztek sputtered across the intersection.

"Hey, Crickett, I don't know what's gone on between you and Charlie Bergstrom, and I don't need to know. I just think you were a little hard on the guy. Regardless of the history between the two of you, the man had just identified his murdered son. Probably not his best day, and I'm thinking you maybe could have cut him some slack."

"Well, maybe he should have thought about that before he decided to act like such a jerk toward me. Stupid Daryl screws up a simple little assignment and the next thing I know Oliver and I are in mortal danger. Drive from point 'A' to point 'B', how tough could it be? But dumb shit Daryl thinks he's gonna play the hero, then instead he screws everything up. No real surprise there," she said, then fumed and crossed her arms as she stared out the window.

"Of course I'm sure Mr. I'm-So-Perfect-Charlie blames me for the whole thing. He said he's going to file for sole custody, make me move. Seriously? And now I'm supposed to play nice? I don't think so."

"What? Crickett, I'm not sure what you're talking about and I don't really need to know. I'm just suggesting that under the circumstances, well it never hurts to be polite and…"

"Whatever! Polite. I'm the one with the baby here, Dev. I'm the one who got nothing but grief from dumb shit Daryl since the day he rolled off me. Good riddance is all I can say. And if that bastard Charlie wants to take me to court, I don't care how much money he has, he's gonna wish he never crossed me. I know people. You want to take Charlie the creep's side, that's just fine. See if I care. Jesus, I tell you what, just pull over and let me out."

"Crickett, I'll drive you home. I was just suggesting that maybe…"

"Pull over, Dev, I want to get out. Now, damn it, pull over," she said and grabbed for my keys.

I slapped her hand away. She hit me on the shoulder and reached for my keys again.

"What the hell do you think you're doing?"

"I said let me out, let me out now," she screamed and started to open the car door.

I felt like stopping right there in the middle of the street, but I pulled across a lane of traffic and skidded to the curb.

"Fuck you," she screamed, then pushed the door open with enough force that it bounced back, and slammed into her ankles, as she was sliding out of the passenger seat. "Ahh-hhh, damn it, you did that on purpose. God I hate you," she shouted, then hobbled onto the sidewalk.

I accelerated away from the curb, reached over as I picked up speed and pulled the passenger door closed, then hit the lock button. My heart was thumping, and I could feel the adrenaline coursing through my body. I could see her in the rearview mirror red faced, giving me the finger, and screaming obscenities at the top of her lungs. A couple of the drivers around me seemed to back off so I would get ahead of them. I took a right on the very next side street.

Three blocks down, I pulled over and began to calm myself. I thought for half-a-second about going back to get her and make sure she was alright. That idea quickly passed. Instead, I decided to drive back to the Medical Examiners, and check on Charlie Bergstrom.

I pulled into the parking lot and back into the space I'd vacated not fifteen minutes earlier. Charlie's red pickup truck was still in the 'Family Parking' space. I decided to just wait for him outside. He didn't need me adding any more trauma to an already bad day.

It was another half-hour before Charlie came out the door. He ignored my car, or more likely he didn't even know it was me.

"Charlie, excuse me, Mr. Bergstrom," I called.

He turned in my direction with a look on his face that suggested could things possibly get any worse? Then he simply stood his ground as I approached.

"Mr. Bergstrom, I just wanted to offer my condolences, well and to see if there's anything I could do for you."

"Do for me? I just lost my son, you think you can make that right?"

I sort of shrugged, and didn't know what else to say. I mean, he had a pretty good point.

"Look, I'm sorry. It hasn't been my best day. Tell me your name again."

"Haskell, Dev Haskell. Please, call me Dev."

"Okay, look, Dev. I'm really pretty overwhelmed at the moment. This whole affair, it's just the logical conclusion to a series of really bad choices Daryl has been making."

I nodded and pretended like I understood.

"Seeing her here, your friend, Crickett. She's just another bad choice in Daryl's long list of bad choices. Anyway, look, not your problem. Like I said, not my best day."

"Mr. Bergstrom…"

"Please call me Charlie."

I nodded, "Okay, Charlie. Can I buy you lunch?"

"You think that would help?"

"Could it hurt?"

Chapter Eight

It was close to three in the afternoon, we were one of two tables lingering over lunch at Shamrock's. We were seated at a high table, sitting on stools with no one in earshot. I brought another round of beers back to our table, and slid the pint glass across the table to Charlie. He was sort of absently twirling a French fry through a large puddle of ketchup and a million miles away.

"Thanks," he said, but didn't bother to look up.

"So you were telling me about Daryl being an honors student," I said climbing back onto my stool.

He pursed his lips and shook his head. "Yeah, of course that was high school. He earned a scholarship to the U. Things seemed to be going pretty well up until his mother died. Car accident, drunk driver. One minute she's got our lives all organized, the next she's taken from us, that fast," he said and snapped his finger. "Middle of Daryl's sophomore year, his grades just went down the drain. He got involved with the wrong crowd, including what's her name, your friend, Crickett. She was probably ten years older and a good half-dozen lifetimes in experience." He looked up at me and held my gaze.

"I knew her a while back. To tell you the truth I hadn't seen or heard from her in a long time. Well, that is until she sort of ran into me the other day and asked about getting the charges against Daryl dropped."

"And could you, get them dropped?"

"I don't know. I never got that far before, well before things ended up the way they did. The little I know, in all honesty, it may have been a set up. Probably was, but they got Daryl on tape climbing into the van, driving it to the parking ramp. That size of a bust, and under the circumstances, it's pretty hard to think he would have a lot to bargain with other than a name. They wanted him to name someone, make a deal. I have to say all the cards seemed to be in the prosecutor's hands. Still, I thought the least I could do was to see if he could get a fair shot."

He nodded. "The name Ben Gustafson mean anything to you?"

"Any relation to Tubby?" I half joked.

"I think he's his son," Charlie said, then stared at me like he knew a lot more than he was letting on, and didn't as much as blink.

In the cesspool below polite society, there were three givens in St. Paul. Tubby Gustafson had a bad side, no one wanted to be there, and if you were there, it never seemed to work in your favor. Rumor had it, he was involved in everything from women and gambling to drugs. The problem was that's all it had ever been, just rumor. Tubby Gustafson was not the sort of person who encouraged talking behind his back.

"And this Ben, Tubby's kid, he was a friend of Daryl's?"

"The two of them flunked out together. I mentioned getting in with the wrong crowd, Ben supplied Daryl with drugs, introduced him to Crickett, and in general was one of the major reasons we are here today." Charlie spread his hands palms up as if to say, *'isn't it obvious?'*

"Ben Gustafson was the one and only bargaining chip Daryl had. I'm pretty sure the cops knew it, probably just wanted Daryl to confirm what they already knew. He tried to play the hero, it didn't work, and the rest is just, well here we are," Charlie said then he followed with a healthy swallow from his pint glass. He stared off into space and slowly shook his head.

"Did Daryl tell you that?"

He shook his head. "Hell no, those two fools, Daryl and that idiot, Crickett. The first I heard about any of this was the call from the police this morning telling me there had been an incident. An incident, Jesus Christ."

"You didn't happen to stop over there this morning for breakfast or coffee to give her the news, did you?"

He absently shook his head. "No, I phoned, had to even though it's my house. She told me a while back never to come over, then made some stupid threat about a restraining order. I decided it was just better for all involved, Daryl, me, the baby, if I kept a low profile. I suppose I'll have to crawl through that mine field in the not too distant future, damn it."

We sat in silence for a while until I finally asked, "And you know it was Ben Gustafson that asked Daryl to drive the van?"

Charlie seemed to study me for a long moment then shook his head slightly, as if he reconsidered whatever his original intent had been. "I'm pretty sure he was involved. Tell you the truth, right now I really can't see much past getting my son buried next to his mother. Beyond that, maybe I'll try and rescue that little guy, Oliver. Maybe I can get him on a safer path. He doesn't have a snowball's chance in hell the way things stand right now. Look, thank you for lunch. Sorry we met under these circumstances, but if you'll excuse me, I've got a pretty full plate just now." He reached over and made a grab for the bill.

I got there first. "No, I said I'd get it. I appreciate your time, Charlie. Look, if I can help you out in any way, please give me a call," I said, and then pulled a business card out of my wallet and handed it to him.

He took the card, nodded, then pushed his stool back and walked out.

Chapter Nine

"God, and I thought things were fucked up before. How in the hell did you get involved?" Aaron LaZelle asked.

I was sitting across the booth from him in The Spot. He was nursing the same Diet Coke that I'd bought him three beers ago. Aaron is a lieutenant in homicide. A rising star, a force to be reckoned with, a man with a bright future, he was also my childhood pal. Oh well, three out of four ain't bad.

"I'm sort of involved through the back door. I was supposed to find evidence that would get all the charges dropped against Daryl Bergstrom."

"Sounds like wishful thinking from what I understand," Aaron said.

I nodded and followed up with a healthy sip of beer. "Maybe more like 'Mission Impossible'. I barely got started when this happened. Sounds to me like the kid was just in way over his head."

"You see the surveillance tape yet? They had him nailed before he even got started. Then this incident happens. Idiots, I would have had him in protective custody from the get go. Who the hell was his attorney? There had to be talk of a deal going down, threats on the girlfriend and the baby. A bust of that magnitude, five million and everyone is asleep at the switch. You gotta be kidding, Jesus."

"You're asking me, Aaron? His attorney was a public defender. Name Daphne Cochrane ring any bells?"

"Are you kidding, that woman? God, we look forward to a victory party whenever she's involved. There's part of your answer right there," he said.

"Yeah, and rumor has it the other half of the answer is Tubby Gustafson."

"Tubby. You're kidding? Who did you hear that from? He usually isn't that close to this type of action. God, I'd love to get my hands on that bastard."

"Well, don't hold your breath, the word I have is it was actually Tubby's kid, Ben. Apparently he was pals with the Bergstrom kid."

"Nice pal. From what I hear young Ben is supposed to be the heir apparent, but he's not the old man. His reputation is the kid's always stepping in it. Then Tubby has to come to the rescue and clean up the mess."

"I'm guessing someone was afraid Daryl Bergstrom was going to give up Tubby's kid in exchange for a deal and well," I shrugged to suggest the obvious.

"And you know this how?"

"Daryl Bergstrom's old man, Charlie. I met him, talked with him over lunch. It's a comedy of errors, a mixed up kid making a number of bad choices. Someone panics and the next thing you know he's dead. Anything you can tell me on your end?"

"About the murder? We've got it all on tape, repeat offender, about a ten-time loser. The Bergstrom kid's throat was slit with a piece of glass if you can believe it.

Some perennial loser named Duncan Nixon. Got a list of priors longer than your arm. It looks like he was locked up on some domestic charge within twenty-four hours of the Bergstrom kid getting arrested. I'm guessing he was in there just in case the option was needed and, apparently someone thought it was."

"I saw Daryl Bergstrom at the Medical Examiners, he looked pretty beat up."

"You were at the M.E.'s?"

"Just holding a hand, which didn't seem to work any too well. The Bergstrom kid had a big bruise on the side of his face. No makeup on him so it was a pretty tough deal for the old man."

"Yeah, the whole thing, the assault I mean, probably took all of ten seconds. Kid gets blind sided with a knockout punch walking out of the shower, carotid artery slashed before he was on the floor. Two uniformed deputies within twenty feet, and by the time they subdue that Nixon douche bag, the Bergstrom kid has bled out on the floor. No real surprise other than I wish someone, somewhere would have put two and two together and gotten that kid into protective custody. Christ, they had him wandering around in the general population, he was clueless."

"Like I said, Daphne Cochrane. I'm told she just shrugged off any concern about Bergstrom's protection. There was a death threat of some sort on his girlfriend and their baby, too. Apparently she blew it all off."

Aaron gave a long exhale and shook his head. "Jesus. So who were you working for? The Bergstrom family?"

"Client privilege, buddy. Not that it really matters, now. I'm guessing I'm off the case before I even get a billable hour racked up."

"Just watch yourself, Tubby gets wind of you getting involved in any way and there's a real potential for problems."

"I'll just have to remember to shower alone from now on. I'd still like to see the tape, both of them actually, the arrest and the murder."

"I can get you in, but does the term 'air tight case' have any connotations?"

"Yeah, I know. I'm just curious and want to see it for my own prurient interest."

Chapter Ten

I was in a viewing room on the third floor of the police department. 'Room' was the operable word. The thing was about half the size of a standard broom closet. It housed a small desk, an overhead ten watt bulb, and an ancient computer running Windows XP as the operating system. Given the city's current budget restraints, I was lucky there was even electricity in the room.

Aaron's description of 'air tight' didn't do the tapes justice. Along with the police tape of Daryl Bergstrom pulling the keys out from under the floor mat of the van, driving for twelve minutes, and parking on the upper floor of a parking ramp, there was the grainy tape from the undercover vehicle following him. The tape from the parking ramp security camera was a four-second delay series of images that piled on additional credibility to the charges, not that any was needed.

The actual tape of Daryl's murder from the county jail a few days later was so short I had to replay it a half dozen times. Aaron showed me the evidence bag with the piece of glass used to slit the kid's throat. My guess and the assumption of the police was it had been brought in by Duncan Nixon forty-eight hours earlier for that express purpose. That led to some obvious questions, for starters, why? What was in it for Nixon? It was pretty obvious he wasn't going to get away with the murder. In fact, once he slit the kid's throat, he stepped back, and calmly called the deputies over to watch. He'll get life with a possible parole after maybe thirty years, but at age forty-six there's a pretty good chance he'll never make parole.

That brought me back to Daryl Bergstrom. Who, in their right mind takes a hundred bucks from someone to drive a van into a parking ramp, and apparently doesn't ask any questions? Wouldn't you maybe just glance under one of the tarps in the back of the thing out of normal curiosity? Was the kid that stupid or was there more to this?

"Your time's up here, Haskell, I need this room," Detective Norris Manning said as he pulled the door open in the viewing cubicle. It was one of life's great mysteries. I'd thus far been unable to figure out what I'd ever done to him to get the attitude. I figured he was probably doing his level best to link me to Daryl Bergstrom's murder before I even asked to review the tapes.

"I'll be finished in just a minute. I want to rerun this detention tape once more and…"

"What part of 'time's up' isn't getting through your thick skull? I just told you I need this room now, official business."

"Manning, you got four viewing rooms, the other three are empty. Why do you…"

"Because I like this one. Now shut that thing off and let me get back to department business."

"Hey, what the hell is it with you, Manning?"

"Me?" He cracked the ever present piece of gum, bit it actually, probably imagining he was taking a bite out of me. "Let's just say I like the taxpayers of this city to get the best value for their hard-fought dollars. That would seem to leave you out, unless of course we're putting you behind bars. Now, if you don't mind, I've got some viewing of my own to do."

"Kids stealing candy?"

"Cute, real cute. Get moving."

I ejected the DVD from the ancient computer.

"I'll take that, no telling where it will end up otherwise," Manning said and reached for the DVD.

I beat him to it, and placed it back in the plastic case before he had a chance to recover. "Not a problem, besides I'm the guy signed out on this and I wouldn't want to disappoint your boss, the good lieutenant."

"Move out."

"As always a unique pleasure, Manning, enjoy your day," I said and left.

On the way to my car I was thinking; on the one hand Duncan Nixon would be the guy to talk to, on the other, why bother? I didn't have a horse in this race.

Chapter Eleven

The flop house over on the East side had faded gray aluminum siding and a substantial number of serious code violations, not the least of which appeared to be renting rooms without being classified as a rental property. From what I could determine, Destiny Meyers apparently shared a room with Duncan Nixon, and probably just about anyone else who could meet her hourly rate. She gave a resigned sigh, took another long drag off her cigarette, and looked at the drink in her hand.

"I told you on the phone, he ain't here," she said then emitted a cloud of blue smoke that seemed to hang between the two of us. She rattled the ice cubes in her glass to accentuate the point of his absence, then stared at me dead pan while she took a healthy gulp.

She looked old beyond her thirty-something years. The lingering traces of a black eye, and the faded yellowish bruise on her cheek did nothing to help. She leaned against the doorway at the end of the hall, drained her drink then finished off with a satisfied gasp. It wasn't quite ten-fifteen in the morning.

"That's why I thought it might be a good idea to talk. I don't think Mr. Nixon is going to be coming home anytime soon. I just have a couple of questions to ask you, background information is all."

"Am I gonna need a lawyer? 'Cuz I ain't got that kind of cash. God, I told you guys everything I know. Why do you keep bothering me?"

"I promise it won't take more than a couple minutes. Could I come in? Or, if you like we could just talk out here in the hallway." The door to the next room was wide open. When I had walked past, the occupant had appeared to be either passed out or dead on the floor.

"God, I 'spose, come on in. Just make it fast. I got shit to do. You want one?" she asked rattling her ice cubes again and maybe suddenly thinking more along business lines.

"Thanks, but I better say no."

"You sure? Never know what could happen," she said then held the door open with her foot just long enough for me to step in.

"No, I better take a pass, but thanks for the offer."

"Fine, be that way." She shrugged, then reached into a Styrofoam cooler sitting on the floor, and tossed an ice cube into her glass. She grabbed the half-empty fifth of Old Fitzgerald next to the hot plate on the dresser and filled her glass a healthy two-thirds full, then turned and tried to look seductive while she sipped. It wasn't working.

"Look, Miss Meyers, I..."

"Call me Destiny, who knows we might become good friends." She smiled, then pulled a folding metal chair back from the card table and sat down. She pushed the pizza delivery box onto the floor and casually tossed a pack of cigarettes in front of her.

"Okay, so I'll tell you what I told the others. What's your name again?"

"Dev Haskell."

"Hmm-mmm, go figure. Anyway, I moved in here with Asshole a few months ago. You could say I was just sort of between things. Thought we might, you know maybe get together on a more permanent basis, only it turns out he was getting the better part of the deal. We were partying that night, he gets pissed off for some reason, and hits me. I told him I was gonna call the cops. He hits me again, I called the cops. You guys come, haul him to jail, where he belongs, I might add. Next thing I know, three or four days later, there's about a hundred of you in here going through all my personal shit and everything, messing the place up. Hell, take a good look around, I haven't even had time to clean up," she said, then drained a good portion of her drink.

A quick glance confirmed what she said. Apparently she hadn't had time to clean for quite a while, but I was guessing months rather than the few days in question. Trash bags were piled against the far wall beneath the faded beach towel hung haphazardly over the window. The clothes on the floor looked about four weeks' deep. The double bed had just one grayed sheet crumpled at the foot of the bed and a sweat stained pillow at the head. Nothing resembling a fitted sheet, or even a pad, covered the mattress. Two bare bulbs hung from the light fixture in the center of the ceiling, one of the bulbs appeared to be burnt out.

"Business must be good," I said.

"Whatever."

"Did he ever mention the guy in jail, the kid he killed?"

"I'll tell you the same thing I told the others, hell no. I never heard him mention that kid. What was his name again?"

"Bergstrom, Daryl Bergstrom."

"Yeah, that's the one, never heard of him before."

"How about someone named Ben?"

She gave me a funny look, shook her head and sipped. "Never heard of no Ben."

"How 'bout a guy named Tubby?"

"Tubby? You mean like fatty? No, that ain't ringing a bell."

"What did Duncan do?"

"Do? God, nothing, bastard didn't do a damn thing. Had my ass out there on the street, didn't care if it was raining, snowing, hot or cold, just told me to get out there and get to work or he'd kick my ass."

"He ever have any friends stop over?"

"For freebies? No, not for a long time, I didn't like that, and put a stop to it."

"How about people stopping over to see him?"

"Who'd want to?" She took another healthy sip. "He'd show up once in awhile with shit, I'm thinking it was always pretty hot, but I never asked no questions. You know, like where he got it and that. Had a flat screen once, but some guy showed up, partied with me for a night then he grabbed the flat screen on the way out the door. Told dumb shit Duncan he'd be back to collect, but I never seen him again. Old Duncan, it scared the crap outta him. He took off for pretty near a week that time. That was kinda nice, actually."

She lit a cigarette and took a long drag then reached up to the dresser behind her for the bottle of Old Fitz and topped off her glass. "Sure you won't have one? I'm kinda getting in the mood," she said then raised her eyebrows implying this could be a good thing.

"I better not. And you never heard him mention Tubby Gustafson?"

"Gustafson? He did something for a Mr. Gustafson a few times, never heard him say Tubby. Who the hell would name their kid Tubby? Jesus, some chicks got their head so far up their ass. I mean, really."

"What did he do for Mr. Gustafson?"

"Tell you the truth, I got no idea. Honest. I just know he didn't try and pull any of his usual bullshit. I never, ever met the guy that I can remember. But he sure as hell had old Duncan scared shitless. Yeah, Duncan wasn't gonna fool with Mr. Gustafson none, that's for damn sure," she said, and then gulped her glass down about halfway.

I began to feel an itching, bed bugs? Some weird skin disease? Just the general filth in this grimy little room? I wasn't sure, but I knew I had to go, and soon.

"Thanks for your time, Destiny. Let me give you one of my cards. and if anything crosses your mind regarding Duncan and Mr. Gustafson, I'd appreciate it if you'd give me a call."

"Will I get paid?"

"Maybe, it depends on what you've got."

"Sure you won't stay, I could show you what I got, it'll be fun," she said then flashed her eyes at me over the rim of her glass.

"Gee, sorry. I'm sure it would be, but I have to run. You think of anything please give me a call," I said, and tossed a couple of my business cards on the table.

"I'll maybe give you a rain check, you're kinda cute," she said. She staggered as she got to her feet, and steadied herself against the edge of the dresser. The bottle of Old Fitz rocked back and forth as I made a hasty retreat for the door.

I fled the scene, and debated about burning my clothes as I drove home.

Chapter Twelve

All that proves is that idiot, Duncan Nixon had a semblance of a brain," Louie said.

We were in the office. I was seated behind my binoculars, scanning the third floor of the building across the street. I'd just finished telling Louie about my Destiny Meyers moment.

"If he's calling him Mr. instead of Tubby, apparently he's not completely stupid. Hey, you seeing anything?"

"Naw, the girls must still be at work." I put the binoculars on the window sill, and spun around in my chair to face Louie. His feet were up on the picnic table, with his eyes closed, his hands rested comfortably across his formidable girth.

"So what's the link between Tubby and this Nixon loser?"

"Link? I think they work in the same industry. Nixon would seem to be a rather unsuccessful member of criminal society, and Tubby is sort of the local CEO of the criminal class. We'll never know, but I'd be willing to bet Tubby told him to get arrested and get access to the Bergstrom kid. In the event Tubby felt threatened, Nixon could kill the kid and problem solved."

"Yeah, maybe, except that doesn't seem to make any sense. Tubby's in the clear. Even if the Bergstrom kid fingers Tubby's son, that's not enough to make an arrest. Five million worth of drugs are in the possession of the police. Bergstroms's nailed and currently lying in the morgue, unable to answer any questions. Nope, there's something else going on."

"Maybe it's just Tubby's general jerky attitude. Even if the kid was set up, at the end of the day he was still the one driving the van when everything went down."

"No question about Tubby being a pain, but the rest still doesn't add up," Louie said then opened his eyes and looked around the office.

"Maybe I should talk to him," I said.

"Tubby? Save yourself some time and just run out in the street into oncoming traffic."

Chapter Thirteen

Rather than run out into the street, I was summoned to appear before Tubby Gustafson in his private dining room, not twenty-four hours later. I'd just arrived stylishly late at the office around noon and climbed out of my Aztek. I was standing in the street, listening to the engine sputter, when a long, black sedan with Limo plates pulled along side and the rear door opened.

"Mr. Gustafson would like you to join him for lunch," some guy said climbing out of the limo. He was tall enough to block out the sun, and looked like he'd have no problem chasing me down, if I was that stupid. He wore a silky purple jacket, and I could see brown leather shoulder straps holding the holster and pistol under his left arm. Under the circumstances, I was in no position to refuse the offer.

Fifteen minutes later, I was on my best behavior, seated across from Tubby at his massive desk I was in a chair so low my chin almost rested on the desk. A linen table cloth was positioned between us. The slabs of fat on Tubby's sides hung heavily over the arms of his chair. He had a round, full face, with a ruddy complexion, topped off with a bulbous nose the size of a baked potato. It would appear his ears, like all of Tubby, had never ceased to increase in size, and the lobes seemed to dangle just above the top of his collar. His hair had been dyed a sort of orangish-ginger tone that from twenty feet away could be spotted as a color not found in nature. It was long, sparse, and greased back against the sides of his skull, allowing the flesh to appear between the slick strands.

I sat and watched as he expertly twirled a forkful of linguine from a large bowl, then washed it down with a red wine whose name I probably couldn't pronounce, and a price tag I certainly couldn't afford. Tubby didn't offer to share.

"I haven't the slightest idea what in the hell you're talking about," he said then slurped more wine. He had a white linen napkin tucked under two of his three chins. He cut a meatball in half, twirled some more pasta then stabbed half the meatball. He crammed the entire mess into his mouth then reached for his wineglass.

It was an intimate meeting, just the three of us, Tubby, me, and Tubby's concierge, a 'gentleman' by the name of Bulldog. Bulldog looked like he hadn't had a positive thought in quite a long time. He had a face that suggested anything you might think of had already been done to it. Judging from the scar tissue around his eyes, and a unique curvature to his nose, I guessed he perhaps wasn't the most affable of individuals. He seemed incapable of a smile, and stood immediately off to my side, maybe a half step behind me. His plaid blazer was a dreadful red and green affair that looked like it had been designed by a sick Scotsman. He wore it unbuttoned, revealing the cross hatched grips of what looked like a .45 stuffed into his waistband.

"So let me get this straight," Tubby said, then stared off into the distance apparently deep in thought. "Some idiot slits another idiot's throat in the county jail, and you think it would be a good idea to mention me and my son as somehow being involved. Is that about right?"

"Well, no sir, not exactly."

"Please, enlighten me," he said, then aggressively stabbed an entire meatball, opened wide, and crammed the thing into his mouth. A mound of red sauce formed on either side of his mouth, which he quickly attacked with his tongue, then grabbed a spare linen napkin off the table and dabbed. He chewed aggressively, turning crimson in the process, and I wondered what would make more sense; attempt a Heimlich maneuver or just watch him choke to death? Unfortunately he swallowed, gasped for air then reached for his wine glass again.

"Well, sir. You see it appears that the individual in question, this guy named Duncan Nixon…"

"Never heard of him. Bulldog?"

Bulldog gave a barely perceptible shake of his Neanderthal skull.

"I was under the impression he may have done the occasional odd task for you. At least that's what I had been led to believe."

"Who the hell told you that?"

"I don't quite recall. I think it might have been one of the detectives downtown."

"Christ."

"Anyway, circumstances would seem to suggest that this Duncan Nixon guy instigated some sort of domestic assault on his girlfriend with the intention of being arrested, put in jail and then placed in close proximity to Daryl Bergstrom."

"The idiot kid who got his throat slit?"

"Yes, sir."

"And my question still stands, what the hell does any of this have to do with me, or my son?"

"Well, sir, ahhh that would seem to be a matter of supposition. See, suppose that Ben, just a thought, but suppose your son Ben sensed from the start something wasn't right with this van parked out there filled with bricks of cocaine. And suppose he maybe offered to pay his friend, Daryl Bergstrom a hundred bucks to drive the van to a parking ramp just in the off chance it was being watched. Daryl Bergstrom gets arrested and is being pressured by the police to give them a name. Of course the only name he had would be your son, Ben Gustafson. So, as a precaution, Duncan Nixon gets himself thrown in jail, and then gets the word, or better yet, decides on his own, it would be a wise decision to make sure Daryl Bergstrom won't give Ben's name to the police."

I sat back and softly exhaled, satisfied I had just finished laying out a fairly accurate, if not chilling rationale to Daryl Bergstrom's murder in the Ramsey County jail.

Tubby sat there and looked unimpressed with my conclusion. He held his fork like he might jump across the desk and stab me. Instead, he nodded at Bulldog to help make his point, then twirled more pasta.

The smack reverberated in my ears, and my head bounced off the edge of the desk. "Ouch, what the..."

"Listen to me, you idiot. Bulldog would like nothing better than a weekend long workout with the likes of you. Just the sort of thing that might improve his attitude and at the same time make my life just a little bit simpler. God only knows why I once again find myself in a generous sort of mood," he said shaking his head. "Here's what you're going to do to help me. You are going to report back to me within the next twenty-four hours. You will have a name or names of individuals falsely linking Ben to this ridiculous drug bust. Next, and more importantly, I want you to find out when those DEA chumps take possession of the drugs from our local police. I don't want that stuff contaminating the good citizens of this saintly city. Do I make myself clear?"

"I can't remember who I talked to on the police force. As for the DEA, they sort of made it pretty clear the last time I was involved with them that they would prefer I just stay away. I couldn't…"

I think Bulldog hit me before Tubby had the chance to finish his nod. It really hurt.

"What the hell part of your simple task do you not understand, Mr. Hassle?" Tubby asked, spitting an explosion of pasta across the table linen in the process.

"Haskell."

Bulldog hit me again, only this time he wrapped his knuckles against the back of my skull which gave off an audible thunk. I saw stars for a moment.

"I'll expect to hear from you within twenty-four hours," Tubby said then crammed another meatball into his mouth. He audibly gulped a good half glass of wine, dribbling onto the napkin beneath his chins in the process. He carefully set the wine glass down then looked up at me, grew suddenly crimson and yelled, "What the hell are you waiting for, get out of my sight."

I was only halfway out of my chair when Bulldog grabbed me by the collar and belt and yanked me up. He marched me toward the doorway picking up speed with every step. At the very last minute, he altered course slightly, and slammed me face first into the door frame. I crumpled onto the floor. My forehead throbbed. My nose began dripping blood down the front of my golf shirt and onto the floor.

"No more than twenty-four hours before I'll expect to hear from you," Tubby called from his table and then sort of toasted me with his raised glass of wine.

Bulldog pushed the door open, watched as I crawled out on all fours, then gave me an encouraging kick in the rear, and yelled, "See 'ya." Then he slammed the door closed behind me.

Chapter Fourteen

"And he was eating spaghetti?" Louie asked then handed me the bag of ice.

"Yeah, well actually linguini with these giant meatballs, and this red sauce all over the place." I gently pressed the ice against the bridge of my nose in an attempt to keep the swelling down. My head throbbed, my eyes were swollen, and in the process of gaining a distinctive purple cast. "But, that's not the point. I'm supposed to *'report back to him'* with some cop's name that mentioned his kid, and then I'm supposed to tell him when the DEA takes possession of the drugs."

"Who's the cop?"

"I made that part up. Actually, I guess it would be Crickett who really told me, but I don't want her mixed up with Tubby Gustafson or his pal, Bulldog. I think I've got an idea on how to deal with that."

"An idea?"

"I'll just tell him that jerk Manning told me."

"Bad idea. Don't you think you're in enough trouble where Detective Norris Manning is concerned?"

"The guy already hates me and besides how's he even gonna find out?"

"Well, he is a detective, and whether you like him or not, he is pretty good."

"Yeah maybe, but I got a tough time seeing him questioning Tubby about me."

"Just be careful, there," Louie said and shook his head. "What's he want to know about the DEA?"

"Not *about* the DEA. He said he wants to make sure they take possession of the drugs or something like that to keep the city safe. Probably doesn't want the competition is what I'm thinking. I'm supposed to let him know when the transfer will happen. Yeah, right, like I'm in the information loop, God, I tell ya." I tilted my head back, closed my eyes and adjusted the ice pack, it didn't seem to help.

"And you're supposed to report back to him?"

"Tubby? Yeah, within twenty-four hours. I'm thinking I might just leave town for a week or two. Take a little vacation."

"You actually think that would work?" Louie asked.

"No."

"So, might there be a backup plan?"

"Not really. I suppose I could warn Crickett. Maybe check with the cops to see if in fact the DEA has taken possession of that cocaine bust. You know, try and get on Tubby's good side."

"You think he even has one?"

"Well, if he does, I certainly haven't seen it."

"Watch yourself, something's up. God knows what, but he's up to something."

"Tubby's up to what he's always up to, no good. You got any aspirin? My head is killing me."

Louie opened his computer bag and rummaged around. He pulled out a couple of cords, a set of head phones, a cordless mouse, and finally an aspirin bottle, which he shook. The thing was empty. "You up for an early afternoon beverage?"

"At this point it can't hurt," I said.

"That's my boy."

Chapter Fifteen

My head was killing me. We'd been in The Spot for barely half an hour and the pounding in my head had gotten worse. It felt like a base drum booming in a small closet.

I drained the last of my Mankato beer, then said, "I'm sorry, Louie, but this ain't really helping. Besides, I think I better touch base with Crickett, and let her know Tubby's asking questions around town. It just might be best to keep things quiet regarding this whole affair."

Louie took a long sip from his drink, basically drained the thing then signaled Jimmy the bartender for another. "My advice, for what it's worth just stay away from her, and Tubby, and anyone else involved. Don't take this on, don't do anything for a fee, pro bono, or for benefits," he said arching an eyebrow.

"How dumb do I look?"

"You mean with the black eyes and that swollen nose? Right now pretty damn dumb."

"Okay, I get it. I'm just going to alert her to the fact that Tubby's looking around for names and tell her to keep quiet. That's all, what could go wrong?"

"Don't even go there," Louie said then nodded thanks to Jimmy as he slid a fresh Jameson across the bar.

I pulled in front of Crickett's house not long after that. It was a little past three in the afternoon. There was a late model gray van parked across the street, and down a couple of doors, with one of those *'Baby on Board'* signs in the rear window. Other than that, the street was empty, well except for the shiny black S65 AMG Mercedes parked in front of Crickett's house. I didn't know what they went for other than it probably cost more than my house. The thing sported a pair of designer license plates that read *'BeniBoy'*.

My Aztek finished sputtering at the curb just as I rang the doorbell. After a wait, I attempted to open the screen door so I could knock, but the door was hooked from the inside. I rang the doorbell again. Crickett finally opened the door after my third ring. She looked glassy-eyed, and spoke to me through the screen door, strongly suggesting there was no way I was going to come inside.

"Oh, Dev, it's just you." She sounded more than a little disappointed.

"Hi, Crickett, mind if I come in?"

"Yeah, actually. See its nap time so we were just about to climb in bed."

"You and Oliver?"

"He's already asleep, and I was going to lay down, sorry," she said and began to close the heavy oak door.

"No, wait, Crickett. Hold on, I just wanted to warn you."

"Warn me?" she scoffed, then said. "And what the hell happened to you? You look like shit. You fall down the stairs or something?"

"Gee, thanks, sorry nothing that dramatic. Look, I've put some feelers out, and at least for the time being, I think it might be a good idea if you maybe didn't mention anything about Daryl, his arrest or anything connected to it."

"I've already moved on from all that, Dev. It's time for me, now."

"For you?"

"Yeah, his funeral is tomorrow. I suppose I'll have to make an appearance, play the grieving widow kind of part, but after that, I just want to get what's coming to me. What's rightfully mine."

"I thought you said he didn't have a job."

"Well, yeah, but there's a trust fund or something, I mean, I think under the circumstances it might be the least he could do."

"He? You mean Charlie Bergstrom, Daryl's dad?"

"Yeah, stupid Daryl's crabby old man. I mean let's be honest, I certainly put in the time, and I had that baby with him and everything."

"Little Oliver."

"Damn right, that little shit's gotta count for something."

"Oliver."

"Exactly."

"Well, I think it might be a good idea to keep it quiet, any talk about Daryl, that is. The less said the better, and it'll only help your cause in the long run."

She nodded in a sort of bored way, then adjusted her stance slightly so she could close the door. "Anything else?"

"Yeah, you know who owns that car, the Mercedes?"

"That black one?"

I looked over my shoulder, other than my car, and the *'Baby on Board'* van down the block, the Mercedes was the only other vehicle on the street. It also happened to be black and parked directly in front of Crickett's house. "Yeah, the one right there, in front of your house."

"Nope, no idea."

"Really," I said and stood there nodding in a way that made it pretty clear I didn't believe her.

"Look, I gotta go, see ya," she said then closed the door, a second later the lock clicked then I heard the chain lock being slipped on.

I pushed speed dial on my phone as I pulled away from the curb and waited. She answered on the second ring.

"Department of Motor Vehicles, this is Donna, how may I help you?"

"Hi, Donna."

There was a painful pause before she lowered her voice, eliminated any prospect of positive thought or attitude and replied. "What the hell do *you* want?"

"I need you to run a plate for me. Shouldn't be too hard, it's personalized. *'BeniBoy'*," I said, then paused a moment before I spelled it out.

She gave an audible sigh, then said, "Okay, hold on I'm doing it now."

I could hear her keyboard clicking in the background.

"Hmm-mmm, seems to be a corporate. That's registered to something called Big Boy Enterprises."

"Does it give a name?"

"I just told you, it's corporate, the name it gives is Big Boy Enterprises."

"I wonder if you could, hello? Hello, Donna?" She'd already hung up on me. There was no point in calling her back, I'd worn my welcome out years ago. As long as I didn't push, I could still make the occasional call, and intimidate her enough to get an answer. Big Boy Enterprises sure sounded like it could be Tubby Gustafson, and 'BeniBoy' sure sounded like it would be Tubby's dumbbell kid, Ben. I figured the kid might be over there giving something more than just condolences to Crickett. That reminded me of the drink glasses, breakfast plates, and two coffee cups, in her kitchen sink the morning I'd rushed over to Crickett's after she's called. It suddenly dawned on me that Daryl had already been arrested and locked up for a few days. So, who was Crickett having breakfast with? I was afraid I may have just found out.

"I told you. I warned you," Louie said. He hadn't left The Spot and was still sitting on the same stool a couple of hours later. "If I recall correctly, I think I said something to you along the lines of staying as far away as humanly possible from everyone and anyone involved in this disaster."

"Yeah, I know, but I'm just curious about what's going on. If she's in tight with Tubby's kid, Ben wouldn't that be a pretty strong indication that Daryl Bergstrom really was set up?"

Louie took a sip and seemed to think about his response. "Yep."

"Well, what does that tell you, man?"

"It tells me this is way more screwed up than either one of us originally thought. It tells me, God bless him, but young Daryl Bergstrom was even dumber than we thought or an awful big risk taker. And, it tells me that the distinct possibility of something going very wrong here is even greater than the one-hundred-percent probability I initially suspected."

"Yeah."

"No, Dev, not yeah. Jesus, what part of stupid don't you get? I'm done talking about this. You know where I stand, I've told you any number of different ways that you're an idiot for getting involved, and so now I don't want to talk about it anymore. Okay? Just let it go and tell me about the latest woman that dumped you or what you got on tap for tomorrow."

"Actually, I was planning to go to Daryl Bergstrom's funeral tomorrow."

"Oh Jesus."

Chapter Sixteen

On a good day Vaxholm, Minnesota was a town of about eleven hundred people. Probably a third of them seemed to have turned out for Daryl Bergstrom's funeral service, and judging from their age, I'd guess most, if not all, were there for Charlie rather than Daryl. Including the pastor's generic eulogy, the service didn't last forty minutes. Coffee and cookies followed in the Princess Amalia fellowship hall.

Crickett was there, too. She wore a very short, very bright red skirt, with very high heels, and a black bra strap that kept falling off her shoulder. She was attempting to hold court, with little Oliver in tow and not meeting with much success. The friction between she and Daryl's father, Charlie, felt palpable, and they inhabited opposite sides of the fellowship hall. Just about everyone was crammed over on Charlie's side. Next to me, I think the only person Crickett spoke with was little Oliver, and he wasn't answering back.

She gave me a long hug, then stepped back once she had people's attention. "Oh God, thank you so much for coming, Dev," Crickett gushed. "Wasn't that just the most awesome service, since forever?"

"Yeah, I guess, I mean I don't really know, I'm not that into funerals. You get your nap in yesterday?"

"I did as a matter of fact. Sorry we couldn't chat any longer, but well," she cupped her hands, looked down at Oliver, and smiled. "Mommy just needed her time in bed."

Nothing positive would be accomplished by me responding. "Hate to hug and run, but I've got kind of a heavy day, Crickett, and I better get a move on. I just wanted to pass on my condolences. Like I said yesterday, maybe don't mention anything for awhile, and just let things sort of cool down."

"As far as I'm concerned, the sooner Oliver and I can put this whole awful affair behind us, the better it will be. We're going to have a fresh start, aren't we Oliver."

A couple of women studied us from the far side of one of the cookie platters, and seemed to somehow communicate with one another without uttering a word.

"Yeah, well I'm going to just pass on my condolences to Charlie, and then I'm heading back down to St. Paul. It's been nice to see you again. Sorry it was under these circumstances."

"You mean you're leaving? Already?" she said and glanced over toward the crowded side of the fellowship hall.

"Yeah, I better get back I've got a lot going on."

She gave me a long stare, suggesting she couldn't believe it then said, "Suit yourself."

On some other day with some other person, I may have tried to explain and smooth things over, or just flat out lied. I figured with Crickett that was as good as it was going to get, and so I just smiled, nodded, and beat a hasty retreat through the crowd on Charlie's side of the room. I had to stand and wait while he finished talking to three or four people, then he turned and got a hug and a kiss from two women.

"Mr. Bergstrom, Dev Haskell, I just wanted to say how sorry I was, and to wish you the very best."

He studied me for a long moment. The swelling on my nose was gone, but my eyes were still rimmed in fading purple. He extended his hand. "Thanks, it's been a long week."

There followed a long pause fortunately brought to an end by another couple tapping him on the shoulder. He nodded at me before he turned to face them, and I took that as my cue to flee the scene.

I was just crossing back into the city limits, when my cell rang. "Haskell Investigations."

"Mr. Gustafson wants to see you, now."

I guessed it was Bulldog, and wondered who had helped him dial the phone. "Gee, my last visit ended on such a pleasant note, I think I'll take a pass. You can tell him the cop who spoke with me was Detective Norris Manning in homicide. I can't get an answer from them on what the DEA is up to. Nice chatting," I said and hung up.

I drove past my house, but didn't see anyone who looked like they were in Tubby's employ waiting for me. I drove down to the office, Louie wasn't there, but his computer case sat on the picnic table, so I figured he might be over at The Spot.

I was right. He was hiding behind an open newspaper, and apparently not on his first beverage.

"So, busy day?" I said climbing onto the stool next to him.

He lowered his paper, looked me up and down, then took a sip. "All dressed up and nowhere to go?"

"No, just got back from that Bergstrom kid's funeral."

He shook his head like he couldn't believe it.

"Will you relax, I was just cutting the cord, making sure I was done with everyone."

"And are you?"

"Mostly, I think, maybe. I gave my condolences and said good-bye to Charlie, the father. Spoke briefly with Crickett, and made it pretty clear I was finished. On the way home, I got a call from one of Tubby's associates. I gave him Manning's name and told him I couldn't get any info on the DEA taking possession. I think that'll pretty much bring things to a close."

"You need a place to stay, tonight?"

"I hadn't thought about that, but it might not be a bad idea."

Louie nodded then slid his glass across the bar. "You're buying."

Chapter Seventeen

My phone woke me about ten the following morning. I could hear Louie down the hall in the shower. I was nestled in his duct-tape covered recliner, next to a pizza delivery box, and the better part of a case of empty beer bottles. I'd slept in the clothes I'd worn to yesterday's funeral.

"Haskell Investigations."

"Hope I'm getting you up," the voice said, then followed with the snap from a wad of gum, Detective Norris Manning. "It's been suggested you might like to grace us with your presence, oh say in the next forty-five minutes."

"What?"

"Just get down here. Amazingly your name has come up in an ongoing investigation."

I figured Manning must have gotten wind of the fact I passed his name onto Tubby Gustafson. Now I was going to have to spend the better part of the next few hours denying that fact. At that point, Louie waddled out of the bathroom, and toweled off more or less in front of me. Things seemed to be going steadily downhill.

The interview room consisted of cinder-block walls painted neutral gray. I was seated at a scratched and cigarette scarred Formica table on a nuclear orange plastic chair. I wasn't cuffed or shackled, not that Manning wouldn't have enjoyed that. I'd already been in here for the better part of an hour cooling my heels, when Manning strode in with a file under his arm.

He attacked the ever present wad of gum with his front teeth. There was a fringe of reddish hair wrapped around his pink dome, and unpleasant past experience had shown me that his icy blue eyes could grow even colder. He tossed the file onto the table, pulled out his chair, and sat down. He took his time opening the file, then straightened the edges, and aligned it with the edge of the table just because he knew it would drive me nuts.

I tried not to react which made him take even more time. Finally I asked, "So, Detective Manning, to what do I owe the pleasure of this meeting?" I was hoping he'd tell me one of Tubby's thugs let the air out of his tires, or lit a paper bag full of dog shit on his front steps. Instead, he pulled a small plastic bag from out of the back of the file, and placed it in front of me. "What can you tell me about this?"

The bag contained a business card that read, 'Haskell Investigations, Devlin Haskell Chief Investigator,' my office address and phone number were printed just below my name.

"Okay, you got me, it's mine. I confess. What's the charge, littering?"

"Always gotta be the wiseass, don't you, Haskell. We pulled this off one of your clients. A little higher up the food chain than the normal lowlifes you seem to be most comfortable dealing with."

"Oh really, who was that?"

"A gentleman by the name of Duncan Nixon."

I think I did a double take. I must have because Manning half tilted his head and reappraised me.

"You mean the guy that slit that Bergstrom kid's throat while in custody? How the hell did he get my card?"

"That's what I was going to ask you."

"What did he say?"

"Gee, you know I asked him, but he seemed to be having trouble speaking. I don't know, it may have been the belt around his neck and the T-shirt crammed into his mouth. What do you think?"

"What?"

"An apparent suicide."

"Two deaths in your facility in the same week. Is anyone on duty down there? A T-shirt crammed in his mouth? This wasn't some suicide, Manning. You know that. Hell, the guy was murdered by Tubby Gustafson."

"Oh really? And you know this how?"

"Because Tubby does that sort of shit. Come on, you know as well as I do that he probably did this just to shut Nixon up. "

"Unfortunately, when it comes to factual evidence, we have to adhere to slightly higher standards than you do, Haskell."

I rolled my eyes and shook my head in disbelief.

"So tell me about Duncan Nixon," Manning said.

"I don't know anything. Honest, I never even met the guy. I never met the Bergstrom kid, either, for that matter. Nixon murdered the kid before I even had a chance to talk with him."

"Why were you going to talk with him, Bergstrom?"

"Doing it as a favor to his, what would you call her, his significant other."

"And Nixon?"

"Never heard of him until he murdered Daryl Bergstrom. Once that happened, I knew I wouldn't be able to see him. Didn't you guys have him under lock and key, or on some sort of watch or something?"

Manning ignored my question. "And the girlfriend?"

"Bergstrom's? I knew her some time back. She contacted me after his arrest and wanted me to find something that would get all the charges against him dropped."

"Pretty tall order," Manning replied.

"You're telling me. You saw me in here reviewing those tapes actually, the ones showing him driving the van into the parking ramp. You remember? It was when you so graciously kicked me out of the viewing room the other day. For the record, I still think the kid was just plain stupid and set up. Someone gave him a 'C' note to drive that van into the parking ramp. At this juncture, I don't think his involvement was anything more than that. I don't know any specific history, but I talked to his father, and he alluded to some pretty bad choices being made in recent years."

"The significant other, what was her name?"

"When I knew her it was Karen Riley, R-I-L-E-Y." I spelled it out for him. "I hadn't seen her for close to a year and a half, maybe two years, when she ran into me just the other night. Told me she was calling herself Crickett now, and that her boyfriend or husband or whatever had been involved in this bust and that the drugs had been planted on him."

"Two pallets stacked with about five million in cocaine? It gets pretty tough to plant that much on someone without them knowing."

"Yeah, that's what I told her. Of course there is that mitigating possibility that maybe the individual is a trusting, naive idiot who's just happy to make a hundred bucks, and didn't bother to look under a couple of tarps in the back of the van he was driving from point 'A' to point 'B'."

"You saw the arrest tapes?"

"Yeah, I did as a matter of fact. I'm sure you have, too. Come on, the kid didn't try to run. My understanding is he was unarmed. At best, I'd say he looked confused wondering what all the fuss was about or he was just stupid enough to think he could joke his way out of trouble. Hey look, Detective Manning, when was the last time you heard of someone transporting that much illicit material, and they don't have so much as a sling shot on them? This whole thing, especially that kid's arrest, just stinks and you guys know it. Was he driving? Yeah, obviously. Did he have any idea what he was transporting? I sincerely doubt it. Now it's even more complicated by his murder, a murder that occurred while he was in your custody. One of two murders, I might add."

Manning made a sort of loud exhale, and I figured the entire incident had been nothing but a series of screw ups from start to finish. Aaron LaZelle had alluded to as much the other day, and we were just talking about Daryl Bergstrom then.

"You guys still got that stuff stacked up in the evidence room?"

"Thankfully, the DEA is taking charge of it later this afternoon. They'll put it under lock and key in their facility, eventually dispose of it accordingly," Manning said, absently. He sounded almost relieved before he returned to the task at hand.

"When did you meet with Duncan Nixon?"

"I just told you, I never met the guy. I never met him before and I didn't meet him after his arrest. I did meet with a woman he was sharing a room with. I'd say they had a *'working'* relationship. Her name, or at least the name she gave me is Destiny Meyers, lives over on the East side in some illegal flop house joint. I talked to her for maybe all of ten minutes. I'd say Nixon was pimping her, had her working the street and probably used her for a punching bag from time to time."

"Yeah, we were over there after the Bergstrom thing went down."

"She mentioned that, said you guys tore up the place, and she hadn't had time to clean up the mess."

Manning ignored my comment. "What'd you talk to her about?"

"I wondered if she knew anything about the Bergstrom kid. She told me she didn't. To tell you the truth, I got the impression she would have trouble remembering anything from about fifteen minutes before. She seemed to be on a pretty steep downward slide. You might say she'd hit rock bottom some time ago and seemed to like it there."

"What else did she tell you?"

"Nothing. I did give her a couple of business cards, told her to call me if she could think of anything. I never expected to hear from her, and I haven't. She was pretty out of it when I met with her, and it was just a little after ten in the morning. She even hit on me a couple of times."

"Hit on you? She'd have to be out of it."

I was on my way home from my interview with Manning about an hour later thinking it made more sense to head home, shower, and change clothes. I drove past my place, but kept on going when I saw the car parked across the street from my front door. Some sort of SUV with dark, tinted windows, and the silhouettes of two guys with no necks who looked an awful lot like they might be waiting for me.

I pulled over around the corner and dialed the '*unknown*' number from the day before. Someone grunted after a half dozen rings. "Yeah."

"Let me talk to Bulldog."

"You got me, Haskell. What the hell do you want?"

"I think I got the information you wanted about the transfer of that material into DEA custody. Tell Mr. Gustafson not to worry, the police are turning it over this afternoon, and the DEA is gonna eventually destroy the stuff."

"Mrumph," he grunted and hung up.

I sat in my car for another ten minutes, then drove around the block, and back past my place. The SUV was gone. Maybe they hadn't been waiting for me, and were just two innocent thugs who pulled over to make a phone call. Maybe they were checking their GPS to see where the nearest gym was so they could go lift weights. Maybe, but I doubted it.

Chapter Eighteen

I was online trying to learn what I could about Big Boy Enterprises, the company that held the title to the Mercedes with the BeniBoy license plates parked in front of Crickett's house.

Big Boy's website consisted of a single page listing all sorts of vague enterprises; historic office buildings, restaurants, a couple of bars, two fitness clubs, catering services, along with resort condos in Minnesota, Florida, California, and Las Vegas. I knew for a fact that Tubby owned one of the bars. A number of the properties were classified as being *'In the process of restoration.'* One of them was the address where I'd met Destiny Meyers. Based on what I'd seen, the only restoration going on there had been returning the place back to the days of cave dwellers.

The web sight neglected to mention any of Tubby's brothels, massage parlors, betting sites, nor his alleged drug distribution operation that encompassed a five-state area. I felt reasonably sure the legal end of his business probably laundered the funds from Tubby's illegal undertakings.

I was tempted to fill out the bogus inquiry form on the site, but quickly decided the less Tubby knew about me the better. I still wondered what the relationship was between Tubby's kid and Crickett. If you put those two together as an item, the arrest of Daryl Bergstrom and his subsequent murder in the shower suddenly started to sort of make sense.

I decided to return to Tubby's sleazy *restoration* project over on the East side and see if Destiny Meyers could tell me anything. At the very least, I might be able to confirm she was the one that handed dearly-departed Duncan Nixon my business card.

Given the state of the place, when I pulled up I wasn't too surprised to see someone walking out the front door in a hazmat suit. Based on what I'd seen the other day, we were all lucky there hadn't been something along the lines of an Ebola outbreak at the address. Then I saw the medical examiners van in the driveway parked next to a discarded boat and a collection of aluminum ladders. Suddenly an Ebola outbreak didn't seem quite so funny.

There was a squad car parked across the street, and I saw another one in the alley. An unmarked car was parked on the street directly in front of the place. I pulled in front of the unmarked car, took my '*Police Vehicle Official Business*' sign out of the glove compartment and slid it onto the dash.

As I walked across what passed for the front lawn, a uniformed officer stepped out of the front door escorting a guy whose hands were cuffed behind his back. I nodded at the cop like we were on equal terms and kept moving. He glanced at me as I passed by, but was preoccupied with his charge and kept going. He helped the guy in handcuffs into the back seat of the squad car then talked into his radio. I climbed the front steps and walked in, acting like I actually belonged there.

I walked past the room where someone had been passed out on the floor the other day when I was here. The door was still open, but the room looked empty. There were two figures standing in the dim, trash littered hallway outside Destiny's room.

In the next room a guy was sitting on the bed talking to a uniformed officer. And just as I recognized the back of his bald head, Detective Norris Manning turned around and stared at me. "God, the unfortunate things you see when there are witnesses," he said.

"Nice to see you again, Detective."

"What the hell are you doing in here?" he growled.

"I came to talk with Destiny Meyers. See if she might know who gave my business card to Duncan Nixon. You remember him, he was the second individual within the past week to die in police custody."

Manning shot a quick glance at the officer next to him, then nodded, and the guy got up and walked past me coming just a shade too close and brushing against me.

I ignored the slight.

"Yeah, I certainly don't have a problem with you speaking with Miss Meyers. We all just need to get along, like they say. Come on, I think she's still right where I last saw her," he said then walked down the hall and into Destiny's hovel.

I followed a few steps behind wondering about his change in attitude.

Destiny Myers was sitting up in bed, naked with her legs spread. Her right leg dangled off the side of the mattress at about the knee, her foot was blue. There was a gag over her mouth and her head was tilted back at an angle. Her face was blue around the gag, but not quite as dark as her foot. Her right eye looked swollen like

84

she had been punched, again. Her arms appeared to be pinned behind her back, and there was a syringe hanging from her left arm.

"I'm sorry, was there something you wanted to ask Miss Meyers?" Manning sounded like he enjoyed asking the question. Some guy with a camera and wearing a hazmat suit gave a smile then continued snapping pictures.

"Are, are, Jesus, are her arms tied behind her back?"

"Tied? Oh no, not at all," Manning paused then chuckled. "As a matter of fact they're taped. I suppose that means we'll have to rule this as an assisted suicide. Christ the paperwork."

"Assisted suicide?"

"You got a better idea? Hey wait a minute, didn't you tell me you were in here meeting with her the other day? That might just make you suspect *numero uno*, Haskell. What do you think, Petey? Maybe Haskell here is just returning to the scene of the crime."

"Might be our best lead up to this point," the camera man said then let the camera just dangle around his neck when he turned to face Manning. "I got just about everything. Once the ME guys are finished, I'll do another set of shots, make sure nothing was moved. You gonna need me in the next hour? I'm thinking of grabbing something to eat."

"Go ahead, they'll be back in here in a few minutes."

He gave me a nod and walked out the door. I heard him a moment later talking to someone down the hallway.

"What was with the guy in cuffs being led out? Did he shoot her up?"

"That piece of shit? No, we just happened to run into the bastard. Couple of warrants out for him, parole violation, assault, possession, they'll throw his ass back in for another twenty-four months. Just another little bit of good luck that comes with the job. Well, and getting to see you again, of course."

"How long has she been like this?"

"You know, Haskell I'm not sure how you got in here. Being the nice guy I am, I'm willing to forget it, at least for the moment. Unless of course you're not out of here in, oh say the next five seconds. In which case, I'll have the pleasure of arresting you as our main suspect. You read me?"

"But how long…"

"Four, three…"

"I'm going, Manning, I'm going." I left the room and moved quickly down the hall.

"Always nice chatting, Haskell. Love to hear more when you've got the time," Manning called from the room then laughed.

The ME team passed me as I headed out the front door. I took two steps down the front steps, looked across the street and yelled, "Hey, what the hell do think you're doing?"

The heads on two kids shot up. One of them took off down the street on his bike as the other slid out from behind my steering wheel and ran between two houses. I chased the little bastard just past my car, watched him jump a fence and keep going. There was no point in attempting to pursue.

The lock on the driver's side had been forced open, but it didn't look like they'd had time to do any damage to the ignition. It would have served them right if they'd stolen the Aztek.

Chapter Nineteen

"You hear the news?" Louie asked. He hit me with the question before I even closed the office door behind me.

"No, two little shits broke into my car and tried to steal the CD player, screwed up the entire dashboard in the process, the radio, my speedometer, all the sensors, everything's shot. Christ, I wonder what this is gonna cost me?"

"You catch 'em?"

"No, they took off, the little shits. I didn't think anything was wrong, I mean the ignition looked okay. Course I drove about five feet and realized everything on the dash was toast, damn it. So, what's the news?"

"Someone hit a DEA van. They were transferring some sort of property from the police department to DEA custody. You believe it? Middle of the day, broad daylight and they steal the thing. What's the world coming to, really?"

I thought back to the two guys parked in front of my place and my phone call to that jerk Bulldog. I hadn't passed on that information to him, had I?

"Anyway, sounds like two DEA agents were wounded. Reports right now are spotty, but it's all over the news. I guess they've got streets blocked around town."

"God, I wonder, you don't think it could be the same stash that Bergstrom kid got nailed with."

"You mean the cops still had that stuff?"

"Yeah. I heard it was going to be turned over to the DEA. They were going to take custody of it at some point, I think, maybe even today, but I'm not sure." Suddenly putting a lot of distance between me and my phone call to that jerk, Bulldog looked like a pretty good idea.

"Well, if that's it, someone's gonna find themselves in a world of trouble."

"The two agents, are they gonna be okay?" Experience had taught me that when one of their 'brothers in the fight against crime' was in anyway endangered, law enforcement had a tendency to sort of throw the rule book out the window. I didn't need to be in front of that runaway train.

"Like I said, the reports are spotty. I would say yes, they're gonna be okay. You know how you sort of get a sense of impending doom with stuff like this? Well, that doesn't seem to be the case, here. Still, anything could happen. Just damn glad I'm not involved," Louie said.

I found myself wishing the same thing. I didn't want to be associated in any way, shape, or form. Thankfully, the odds that my phone call to Bulldog could somehow be traced were slim to none.

"Is it your turn to buy?" Louie asked later. We'd gone into The Spot for just one and had somehow managed to fritter away the better part of the late afternoon.

I honestly couldn't remember whose turn it was, but I liked the idea of Louie paying. A regular we both knew as Teddy came through the side door and shouted out his order to Jimmy, who was chatting with another regular at the far end of the bar.

"You two hiding in here?" Teddy asked, giving both of us the once over.

"Avoiding life's problems," Louie said then took a sip from his glass.

"No, I mean the cops. Least I figured they were looking for you guys. They're all over your place across the street. You still have an office over there?" he said, then nodded thanks to Jimmy as he slid a pint glass across the bar.

Louie and I bolted off our stools, and stared out the small octagonal window that housed the bar's red neon *'open'* sign. There were three squad cars parked haphazardly in front of our two-story building, with their flashing lights still on. One of the squad cars had pulled in against the traffic flow, partially blocking the lane, and leaving the impression it had stopped rather quickly. Four or five people had gathered on the sidewalk across the street watching, a couple of people were out on their front steps further up the block. The occasional passing car slowed to a crawl then gawked as they crept by.

A large, black, uniformed sergeant stepped out of the doorway, talking into the microphone attached to his shoulder. He nodded a couple of times, obviously listening to some sort of response. My cell rang, and as I instinctively reached for the phone the sergeant across the street slowly turned his head in the direction of The Spot. In a matter of seconds five officers were headed across the street. They didn't run, but they weren't wasting time either. Two of the officers cut at an angle across the street and headed for the side door.

"Oh, shit," Louie said and absently backed up a step or two. I headed for the men's room.

89

A moment later I heard booming voices out in the barroom, someone shouted, "Hands on the bar where we can see them." I had just forced the window open in the handicapped stall. I swung my legs out the open window, and dropped maybe five feet to the ground. I sort of banged the side of my face against the exterior, but didn't have the luxury of time to worry about it. I was up and running down the alley in seconds.

I had parked the Aztek under a large elm on the side street, just around the corner from our office. I jogged down the block, then crossed the street, and cut up the alley to get to the Aztek. I slipped behind the wheel, turned the car on then calmly took a left up Randolph heading in the opposite direction from The Spot. I scanned the rearview mirror, but couldn't see anyone in pursuit. They must have still been sorting out Louie and the rest of the beverage clientele inside The Spot.

I couldn't think of anywhere else to go so I drove to Crickett's. The black Mercedes with the 'BeniBoy' license plate was parked in front of her house and I pulled in behind it. I rang the doorbell three separate times, but no one answered. After the second ring, I thought I may have heard voices coming from behind the door, but I couldn't be sure and didn't have the luxury of time to find out so I left after a few minutes.

Chapter Twenty

"Oh really, what sort of trouble are you in now?"

"Why do I always get the third degree from you when I try to do something nice?"

"Maybe because whenever you want to come over to see me it turns out your hiding from someone or you're dodging some responsibility," Heidi said.

"No, it's nothing like that, honest. I just haven't seen you, thought it might be fun to get together. Look if you're busy or seeing someone, I'm cool with that. We're both adults. Sorry I bothered..."

"I didn't say you couldn't come over, it's just that, well admit it, if you were me you'd be suspicious, too."

"No, I wouldn't. If I were you, I'd be wondering what sort of bottle of wine kind, wonderful Dev could bring me."

"Stop it, possibly two bottles might work better," she said.

"I'm there in fifteen minutes."

"Make it thirty, so I can get things set up and just come on in, I'll leave the door open" she said, and hung up.

I sat back in my seat and watched her front door. I was parked about a half dozen doors down the block, and I wasn't going to take any chances. Between the police at The Spot, and the 'BeniBoy' Mercedes at Crickett's, I wasn't sure who I could trust. I waited forty-five minutes just to be on the safe side, then walked up to her front door and let myself in.

The lights were off, and the living room was dark, but there were a half dozen small votive lights burning down the hallway. I went into her kitchen, placed one of the wine bottles in the refrigerator, and opened the other. I poured two glasses, tucked the bottle under my arm, and followed the votive lights into Heidi's bedroom.

"God, it took you long enough." She was lying seductively in bed with a sheet casually draped over her hip.

"I wasn't sure you wanted to see me. You didn't seem that interested and I..."

"Shut up and get in here. What kind of wine?"

"The Vino Verde, that Portuguese stuff you like."

"Perfect."

We were more than halfway through the second bottle. I'd just topped off our glasses and put the bottle back in the refrigerator when she asked, "Okay, so really, what kind of trouble are you in?"

"Heidi, honest, why do I have to be in trouble to want to see you? Can't you just accept the fact that..."

"No, not when you call me from down the street, then wait the better part of an hour before you come in. I know you, Dev something's up. What is it?"

"I wasn't down the street, I was..."

"Dev, I saw you, saw that dreadful car of yours. I was still on the phone with you and looked out the window, and I could see you parked down in front of the Miller's. The only person you're fooling is yourself. You don't want to tell me, fine. But don't lie to me."

"I'm not lying, and it wasn't an hour, you said thirty minutes, I gave you a couple extra, maybe forty, thought you might need it."

"It was forty-five."

"But it wasn't an hour."

"Okay," she said, then waited quietly.

"Well, there's maybe a little bit of a slight misunderstanding…" I went on to tell her what little I knew, the more I talked, the less I seemed to really know.

"So, you know or at least you're awfully sure the police are probably looking for you. And you think they traced you to The Spot using your phone, right?"

"Yeah, I'm pretty sure of that, at least it seemed that way."

"Where's your phone now?"

"Um, kind of at the foot of your bed."

Heidi reached over and took my glass of wine then said, "I think it might be a good idea if you got rid of that. And, while you're at it, maybe pull your car around the block, or at least into the alley."

"I don't think they'll call, it was just so close to…"

"Get. It. Out. Of. Here."

"Okay, okay, I'm getting dressed."

"You can get a new one tomorrow."

I called Louie on the way to toss my phone into the river. He answered on about the eighth ring. I actually was getting ready to leave a message when he said "Yeah."

"Louie, Dev."

"Where are you, man?"

"Never mind. How'd it go at The Spot?"

"They were looking for you. Asked us some questions then sent everyone home, made Jimmy close for the night. They were pretty serious, Dev. I'd watch out. Where the hell are you?"

"About to get rid of my phone. I'll get a new one tomorrow, but I don't need them finding me right now. Did they say what they wanted?"

"With you?"

"Yes, with me."

"No, but they were awfully serious."

"This is tied in with that butthead, Tubby Gustafson, I just know it."

"What are you doing with him?" Louie asked.

"That's just it, not a thing. I want to be as far away from that guy as possible."

"Well, you better think of something, and fast. They weren't fooling around and you've got the DEA joining in. No offense, but probably be best if we didn't talk."

"Yeah, I get it. Look, man, I'll be in touch," I said, and hung up. Five minutes later my phone was sailing over the railing of the Ford Bridge and into the Mississippi. On the way back to Heidi's, I drove past Crickett's. The Mercedes was still parked out front."

It was daylight when Heidi whispered something in my ear about an early morning meeting, and that the coffee was on then she was out the door. I got out of bed just before ten, and showered. I picked up a pay-as-you-go phone, and called Louie. He had nothing new to add, other than to tell me not to come into the office.

I phoned Crickett and hung up the moment I was dumped into her answering service. The Mercedes was gone from in front of her house when I drove past, so I went around the block, then parked in front, and rang her doorbell. No one answered.

I drove past my house, but it looked like there might be an unmarked car parked two doors down. I couldn't be sure, but decided to error on the side of caution, and just kept going.

Chapter Twenty-One

"So you ended up here?" Louie said injecting a tone of disbelief then took another sip as he looked around. We were seated in a back booth at Charlie's, a very quiet joint on the far side of town. We'd been listening to about a thousand different Bob Seger tunes Louie played, while we waited for the local news to come on so we could get the latest on the DEA robbery. We were the only paying customers in the place.

"I have to keep on the move. Obviously I can't go to the office. I think they've got my house staked out. I was at Heidi's last night, but two nights in a row would be pushing it with her."

"Always room at my place," Louie said.

"Yeah, thanks, but I think it's probably too risky. I don't need you getting in any trouble, besides chances are they just might be watching your place, too."

"Anything I can do to help?"

"Yeah, make a show of not being with me."

The news came on and opened up with *"New Developments in the ongoing DEA investigation"* then they broke for six minutes of commercials. Louie and I slid out of the booth and walked over to watch the flat screen mounted above the bar.

"Can you turn it up a notch? Tough to hear over the music," Louie said.

"You really want to listen to this shit? It's all bad news," the bartender said then picked up the remote and increased the sound.

"Breaking developments in the DEA robbery..." The news report went on to give a summation of the robbery, running yesterday's video of ambulances on the scene and the street blocked off. Then they broke to the tape of a press conference held earlier this afternoon where the police mentioned that a cell phone had been found at the scene of the crime and all leads were being aggressively pursued.

"Shit, that's it," I said.

"That's what?" Louie asked.

"The phone. The one they found at the hijacking of that DEA van. You know what, it's coming together and all of a sudden it all adds up."

"No offense, but what's coming together? You're not making a bit of sense."

"This whole thing, Louie. The cops or rather the DEA is on to the drugs in the van, five million worth. They stake it out to nail the bad guys. Meanwhile the bad guys, or should I just say, Tubby finds someone to drive the van, knowing he'll get nailed and the drugs will be taken into custody."

"And so far this sounds really stupid, Dev."

"The stuff is in police custody until it's transferred back to the DEA. Tubby finds out the transfer time, and steals the van. He gets the drugs or maybe even gets *his* drugs back. Daryl Bergstrom is dead, Duncan Nixon's dead, and Destiny Meyers is dead. No one's left to tie Tubby to the any of this."

"The phone thing still isn't making sense. Why not just go after whoever owns the phone?"

"Fake name, pay-as-you-go, something like that. Hell, I bought one just this morning."

"I'm still not tracking. So, they find the phone and they can't trace the owner, how does that help?"

"They trace the calls on the phone. Find out who called it."

"But, how do they come up with you? You didn't... Oh, you stupid, dumb son-of-a-bitch."

I shrugged.

"Whose phone did you call, who owns the thing?" Louie said and shook his head in disgust.

"Well, it might be a guy named Bulldog. He kinda works for Tubby."

"Bulldog. Smooth move. And so they scan the numbers and your name comes up?"

"Probably. It's all making sense, now."

"Sense? No it's not, Dev. You called this dog shit guy on your phone?"

"Bulldog."

You called him? What on earth for?"

"I might have maybe, heard a sort of rough idea when the DEA was making the transfer, sort of, maybe."

"What?" Louie screamed over Bob Seger.

"Keep your voice down, man."

"Why in the hell would you do that? Call him. It makes no sense. Tubby and his band of merry men get off scot free, at least three people are dead which just leaves you and well, maybe that bug woman with the little kid."

"Crickett?"

"Yeah, that's the one."

"I think she's sleeping with Tubby's kid, so she's safe at least for the time being."

"Great, then that leaves just you."

"Yeah, just me…"

"Perhaps a warning here, my friend, based on what we think has happened thus far. Get on your new pay-as-you-go phone, and call Detective Manning or your pal Aaron LaZelle, then get your ass into police custody while you still can."

"Louie, two people have been killed just in the past week and they were both held by the cops. It's highly possible Tubby is behind one or both of those murders. I turn myself in and all that's going to do is let him know my location for the foreseeable future. Hell, he's probably got some idiot already in jail just waiting for the opportunity to nail me if I show up."

"It seems to me you're running out of options, Dev."

"Humph, it seems to me I ran out of options a while ago."

Chapter Twenty-Two

The door was surrounded by an elegant, and at the same time, rustic front porch with six massive split logs for steps. There wasn't a doorbell, just a heavy, shiny brass knocker hanging in the center of the large oak panel. When I banged the thing I could barely hear the sound from the far side of the door before the echo bounced off the dark pine and birch forest surrounding the log house.

Charlie Bergstrom's place was nothing if not serene. It was also very private, difficult to find, and more than a little intimidating. I waited for what seemed an interminable amount of time before a voice called from behind me.

"Can I help you?"

I turned, and recognized Charlie maybe twenty yards away. He was gazing at me from beneath his Vietnam Veteran cap, comfortably resting some sort of rifle with a heavy duty scope on his right hip. His features didn't soften once he recognized me, but he grunted an, "Oh you," then casually approached.

"Denny Hendle, right?"

"Sort of, sir. It's Dev Haskell, actually."

He shrugged, suggesting it really didn't make a difference, glanced around like he might be checking for accomplices, then said, "Please, don't call me, sir. Charlie will do just fine."

"Okay."

"What are you doing all the way up here?"

"I wondered if we might talk."

"I guessing you've driven all the way up from the cities, and I'm sorry you had to make the trip just to hear me say I don't think there's really anything I'm interested in talking about."

"Could I just take five minutes of your time?"

He gave me a look that suggested I was pushing it, but said, "I'm about ready for a cup of coffee, join me, and I'll give you five minutes. But that's about all."

We were seated on a back deck that ran the entire length of the log home. From this side, the structure seemed a lot larger than I'd originally thought, I guessed close to a hundred-feet long. The deck sported an intricate railing with a grand staircase on either end leading down to the ground level. The entire affair was meticulously stained a honey sort of color. It held a large grill, a couple of tables, lots of chairs, and a bar. I noticed speakers with what looked like cameras mounted along the back of the log home. The deck overlooked a dark forest that gave the impression of going on for miles and miles. I could hear water running in a stream somewhere off in the distance, but couldn't see the stream for the pine and birch forest.

"Really nice out here," I said, and meant it.

"Thank you, my refuge from all the bullshit going on out there," he said, and gave a half nod of his head to indicate the rest of the planet. After a moment, he set his coffee mug on top of the railing, and looked at me. "You said you wanted to talk."

"I'm not sure where, exactly to begin, other than to tell you again, I'm truly sorry about what happened to your son. I suppose you heard about Duncan Nixon being killed in jail."

"Last I heard there was talk of possibly labeling that a suicide."

"There might be talk, but I don't think it'll happen. His roommate, girlfriend, whatever she was, a woman named Destiny Meyers was found dead the other day. Apparent drug overdose rigged to look like an accident, but it appears pretty suspicious. I'm guessing they'll eventually rule both deaths as homicides."

Charlie took a long sip from his coffee mug and stared blank faced, looking unfazed by my information. "Shit happens."

"The other thing I thought you should know is that the wounding of the two DEA agents and the hijacking of that van a couple of days ago in St. Paul, may be related to Daryl's death."

"Oh, really?" Charlie said. Strange, just two words, but when he spoke it sounded almost fake or maybe put on, like he had rehearsed a line in a play then delivered it poorly. I couldn't put my finger on it, but he didn't seem the least bit surprised. I plowed ahead.

"Yeah, I think the contraband being transported by the DEA was the same stuff that was in that van Daryl was driving. My thought is that some group actually planned to have the stuff confiscated by the police. That would essentially keep it safe for a couple of days. Under police care it would have been virtually untouchable, well until it was transferred to the DEA. Then they got hit in broad daylight, and now someone has possession of all that cocaine."

"Any idea who that could be?"

"You mean like a mastermind? No. To tell you the truth all sorts of names are bouncing around out there, some legit, some not a snowball's chance in hell. But I don't know anything definitive. I'm not sure the cops know either."

"So why are you telling me this?"

"Why? That's a good question. I'm not really sure to tell you the truth, other than to just let you know. I'd say from the look of things, your son was most likely set up, probably didn't have a clue what he was getting into. I guess I wanted you to know that much, know he maybe just made a bad choice, but he wasn't a bad guy. And, unfortunately I can't prove it, but I think part of the set up may have been to make sure he never told anyone. I don't know if it was part of the plan or just bad luck, but his court appointed attorney wasn't the brightest, and she should have insisted on protective custody the moment she began representing him."

"That would be Miss Cochrane."

"It would."

"Doesn't really help at this juncture, now does it?"

"No sir, I guess it doesn't."

He turned his head and seemed to study me for a long moment, then his eyes softened. "Where'd you serve, son?"

"Iraq, Afghanistan."

He nodded then stared back into the dark forest.

"What'd you do in Vietnam?" I asked.

"Nothing of interest. Look, safe trip back to the cities, come on, I'll walk you out to your car," he said then picked up both the coffee mugs, and headed across the deck.

He walked me to my car, but it was almost as if he was escorting me off the premises. I slid in behind the wheel and was about to say 'thanks for the coffee'.

103

"You watch your six, son," he said then turned and headed back toward those massive log steps.

Chapter Twenty-Three

I was parked across the street and a few doors up from Crickett's house. I'd been sitting in the dark for a couple of hours, thankfully none of the neighbors had walked past and I hadn't seen any window curtains twitching. I was planning to confront Tubby's kid, Ben, if and when the idiot ever pulled up. It wasn't much of a plan, and I didn't have any idea about what I'd do beyond that. Not for the first time I asked myself, *'What in the hell are you thinking?'*

A little before midnight, two sets of headlights turned the corner and drifted down the street. I slid lower in my seat and stared through the space between the steering wheel and the dashboard of the Aztek. The first car pulled to the curb in front of Crickett's, and parked, while the second pair of headlights seemed to tread water, waiting just a little behind. The lights on the second car bounced off the sleek, polished black body and illuminated a Mercedes hood ornament. I planned to check, but I was willing to bet there was a set of designer license plates that would read *'BeniBoy'*.

Eventually, the driver's door opened on the parked car and a large silhouette seemed to pour out of the front seat. The outline looked to be about as large as

Tubby, and my first thought was that his idiot kid would be dead from a heart attack within the year. Then I realized the fat figure was in fact, Tubby.

He flicked a half-wave to the car waiting behind, then waddled up the walk toward the front door. The door opened as he jiggled up the steps, and Crickett stood there for just a brief moment before she followed Tubby into the house and closed the door behind her. The waiting car moved slowly down the street past me, then turned the corner and disappeared.

Crickett? I wondered what kind of woman would want Tubby tapping her on the shoulder at three in the morning asking if she was awake. I waited a few minutes to make sure the coast was clear then walked over to the Mercedes. Even in the dark as I approached I could see the 'BeniBoy' plates.

Light drifted out from two kitchen windows along the side of the house, and I wandered across the lawn and down a dark, narrow concrete sidewalk toward the rear to get a look. The windows were high and I had to stand on top of the water meter to gaze inside.

Tubby was seated at the kitchen table with his enormous rear hanging over the sides of a wooden chair. The chair looked ready to collapse under his weight. A strong looking drink sat next to the open pizza box in front of him. At the moment he seemed to be focused on cramming a gigantic slice of pizza, about an inch thick into his mouth, in the process ignoring Crickett perched precariously on the very edge of his lap. For her part Crickett nibbled his massive ear, careful not to interrupt the flow of pizza or alcohol.

The windows were closed and I couldn't hear what, if anything was being said. They kept up the routine as Tubby worked his solo way through the large, double everything pizza, Crickett seemed content to continue nibbling Tubby's ear.

The kick to the back of my knees was hard enough to send me skyward and parallel with the ground. I bounced once off the concrete sidewalk just as a boot slammed into my solar plexus and knocked the wind out of me. The back of a heavy heel caught me on the forehead. Just before I blacked out I had a couple of thoughts; *'These guys were really good,'* and *'They seemed to be enjoying themselves'*.

The pressure from the bench vice being tightened on my hand sort of brought me back to the surface. I was partially kneeling on a basement floor against a workbench with my left arm pulled over my head. My hand had been shoved into some sort of vice that at the moment was being tightened just below my knuckles. I prayed that if I just remained still whoever was standing over me would go away. It wasn't working.

"You'd think with a workbench, she'd at least have a skill saw down here," a raspy voice said.

"She don't strike me as the tool type."

"You get in touch with Bulldog?"

"He's on his way."

"Tubby, still here?"

"He got his fat ass out of here as soon as he finished that pizza. I was hoping for an early night, but now we'll probably have to deal with this piece of shit." With that last comment, one of them used their knee to bounce my head off the side of the workbench. I sort of half hung there kneeling on the floor, frantically praying they'd go away when I heard what sounded like a distant door bell.

"That's gotta be Bulldog, go let him in," the raspy voice said. A moment later I was aware of footsteps climbing up the wooden stairs.

I could open one eye and saw a foot-long length of galvanized pipe on the bottom shelf of the workbench. I heard the click of a cigarette lighter, and then the sound of an inhale, as the thug standing over me fired up a cigarette. I reached for the pipe and swung it as hard as I could into the knee next to my head. I felt the flesh tear across the back of my hand clamped in the vice. I swung again as the figure standing over me collapsed to the floor. I think I caught him across the side of his skull, but didn't have the luxury to wait and see. I hit him across the top of his head just to be sure, and he didn't react. I struggled to my feet, loosened the vice on my hand and stepped over the body on the concrete floor.

He was face down and very still. I couldn't tell if he was breathing, and at this moment really didn't give a damn. I did see a pistol tucked into the small of his back, actually secured in a belt holster. I tried to pull the holster out, but my left hand was virtually useless after being clamped in the vice, so I unsnapped the safety strap and pulled the weapon loose. It was a small handgun, black with plastic grips. Not heavy duty, maybe a P22, but it was better than nothing. Just as I made my way toward the stairs I heard voices and footsteps overhead. The door to the basement opened a moment later and I ducked beneath the wooden stairs.

There were two pairs of feet clomping down the staircase. One of the voices half giggled and said, "Haskell an old friend stopped by to see…what the fuck? Ricky? Ricky?"

They were halfway across the basement when I fired. I recognized the boot heel on the first figure and caught him in the back of the knee. "Don't," I shouted at Bulldog, as he reached for the weapon in his waistband. I leveled the pistol and aimed at the back of his head.

He spread his hands out to the side. For a moment his right hand carefully held a pistol between his thumb and index finger before he dropped it to the floor. The creep I shot was rolling from side to side at Bulldog's feet attempting to muffle his screams and grunting. His eyes looked wild and he seemed to be foaming at the mouth.

"I ain't got a gun now, I'm unarmed," Bulldog said.

"Get your ass down on the floor. Stretch out and keep your hands where I can see them. You try anything I will blow what little brains you got all over the wall. Honest to God, I swear I will."

He slowly knelt down on the basement floor, exhaling in protest, like it was one more stupid thing he had to do. As he stretched out, I stepped over and used my foot to slide his pistol further away until I felt comfortable picking it up. My left hand was beginning to function, but I still bobbled the weapon, and had to press it against my hip to hang onto the thing.

"You got any idea the kind of trouble you're in, Haskell. No one does this to Tubby," Bulldog said. "Just where in the hell do you think you're going to..."

"Shut up, Dog Shit," I said, and pushed his face into the gray concrete floor with my foot then I quickly stepped back and kicked him in the ribs. The kick seemed to have little effect other then he growled on impact. I could see his temple flutter as he ground his jaw back and forth. His lower lip curled evilly, and I was sure even now he was making plans for me. His partner had settled down somewhat, and wasn't rolling back and forth although he still held his knee and grunted with each and very exhale.

"I don't want anything from you or Tubby except to be left alone."

"That ain't gonna happen, I just told ya, no one does this to Tubby."

"Looks like I already have. Now you just stay there nice and quiet like and I'll leave. This is my one and only warning. I see either of you get off that floor it's gonna be one of the last things you ever do."

Bulldog shook his head ever so slightly, like he couldn't believe how stupid I was, then mumbled something I couldn't pick up.

"What was that?"

"I said you're as good as dead, Haskell, dead meat, you hear me," he growled, but I was already halfway up the stairs and heading for the backdoor.

Chapter Twenty-Four

"Are they okay? The guy you hit with the wrench, and the other guy you shot?" Louie asked.

"Okay? That's not the point, man. I wasn't about to hang around, and ask to help out. I don't know, and I don't care if they're okay. I left them in Bulldog's caring hands. I just wanted to get out of there in a semblance of one piece."

"Dev, at what point do you get the police involved?"

"Yeah, that's a good idea. Why didn't I think of that? You know, just tell them I happened to be window peeking, and then I assaulted a guy with a pipe, and I think he might be dead. Shot another guy when he ran down the basement stairs to help his assaulted friend, and threatened to kill the bunch of them on my way out the door."

"Well, that's certainly one version."

"Arghhh, Louie. The problem is I told you my version, but that's not what the law is going to think. Hell, they'll lock me up while they sort it out, and I'm convinced that fat ass Tubby has someone already in jail just waiting for me to be locked up so he can kill me."

"There is that," Louie shrugged and took a sip. "So, your plan?"

"Plan? I don't know, possibly relocate to some obscure place, Iowa or somewhere."

Louie shook his head.

"Just kidding, man. I don't know, but I'm sort of officially on the run. I'm sure Tubby has a price on my head by now. He's probably got all sorts of sleaze balls out there looking for me. I can't go home, can't go to the office. It's a pretty safe bet your place and Heidi's are probably being watched. God, even The Spot isn't safe for me right now," I said. I was still stiff after sleeping fitfully in the back of the Aztek. I had a goose egg on my forehead, and my left hand was still sore and a little swollen, thankfully it was working more or less.

"Want another?" Louie asked, then signaled the bartender without waiting for my answer. We were seated on bar stools at Tootsies, just the two of us in the place, well and the bartender, but then again, it was only a little after nine in the morning.

"You got any coffee?" I asked, as he poured me another beer.

"I think there might be some, but it's probably been on since last night, let me check," he said, and pushed the refilled pint mug across the bar toward me.

"Never mind, I can live without it."

"Suit yourself," he shrugged, then sat down on a stool at the end of the bar, and went back to reading yesterday's paper.

"There must be somewhere you can land, maybe just let things cool down. I don't know, what about getting word to Tubby? Maybe tell him you're backing off and gonna forget the whole thing? No offense, Dev, but probably not the brightest idea you've had, hanging around and peeking in the window at that chick's house."

"Oh yeah, Crickett. What a piece of work she turned out to be. And by the way, remember she contacted me, not the other way around. God, and I tried to help. I tell ya, no good deed goes unpunished. As far as getting word to Tubby, maybe that would work, but then there's his lunatic enforcer, Bulldog. Who knows what that animal will do? And by the way, what's with Tubby shacking up with Crickett? Where's his idiot kid, Ben?"

"Maybe he'll forget."

"Tubby?" I gave Louie a look that suggested otherwise.

"So again, you got somewhere you can go where no one would think of looking? God forbid, but have you got anything like a plan?"

"I'm sort of coming up with one. I'm still in the rough outline stage right now."

Chapter Twenty-Five

"**Oh. My. God. Look** who finally came back for more." She giggled then gave me a passionate kiss and an improper squeeze at the front door. "You just get those firm little buns in here. Look who came back to see mommy, kids."

I was really at the end of my rope. Brenda Livingston had been a weekend gone very wrong over a year ago. She stalked me for about four months after that, before directing her attention to some other fool. I swore I would never, ever call her back and now here I was being ushered into her basement apartment. She grabbed my rear, and squeezed as I walked past.

"Ohhh, isn't this going to be fun," she said to the cat she was holding. She wore a black leather vest edged in white lace, and barely held together by just two little buttons. Her tight leather skirt was extremely short, I think I owned belts that were wider. She wore a black garter belt that easily extended four inches below her skirt, and held up her hose that had a seam running up the back, and some sort of floral pattern across her thighs.

When she spoke she used two different voices, one for me, and a high pitched one for her cats. She cradled one cat, but I could see three others, two curled up on the couch, and another one under the coffee table that held a half dozen statues and a couple stacks of 'Precious Moments' collector plates; the kids with the big eyes. There was an end table on either side of the couch, each one had a Tiffany-style lamp sporting butterflies, and lots of little figurines scattered around, more 'Precious Moments' stuff. An oversized painting of two reclining naked guys, clearly excited, hung over the couch. I knew there had to be more cats running somewhere around the place.

"Great to see you again, Brenda, it's been awhile."

"Too long, baby, I've been in heat ever since I got your phone call." Then she switched to her cat voice and said, "Oh, we are all going to be such naughty girls."

I could feel my eyes already beginning to water and my arms were definitely starting to itch. I'd taken four Benadryl on the way over, and stuffed a half dozen more in my pocket. I knew I was bound to need them. I sort of spit a cat hair off my lips, and smiled at Brenda.

"This is Princess Di," she said in that high-pitched voice then held a yellow-stripped cat out in my direction.

I wasn't sure if I should take hold of it or just pet the thing, my nose suddenly began to twitch. "She's just lovely," I said, and stepped over to the dining room table. "Hey, I picked up some wine, if I remember this was one of your favorites." I set the paper bag on another stack of collector plates, and pulled out one of four bottles, then opened up a second bag and brought out a little rubber mouse with a bell on its tail. "And, well I figured I better get something for all your friends to keep them happy."

"Oh, that's so sweet. Yes, because you and I are going to be *busy*, Mister." She pointed first to me, then herself as she said *'you and I'*, then she ran her nails across my chest and growled.

She picked up the rubber mouse, placed it in her mouth, and switched personalities again. "Look what he brought for us, who wants to play?" she squeaked then shook her head from side to side making the little bell ring. The cats couldn't have been less interested.

"Princess Di? Come on, sweetie, come get it. Good, good, that's my girl yes, yes right under the couch. Oh, you little darling."

There was a box of Kleenex nestled between a half dozen wide-eyed, red-cheeked dolls on a bookcase. I pulled a piece out of the box to blow my nose, but I think I only succeeded in rubbing more cat hair onto my face.

"Bring that wine into the kitchen, Dev and let's get this party going. I've got a wonderful eggplant dish I know you'll just love, I've gone Vegan, darling."

I followed her into the kitchen where the table was set for two. A large, unlit candle emblazoned with gold angles sat in the middle of the table, and a gray-striped cat walked back and forth across the dinner plates. Brenda ignored the cat and lit the candle. She took two wine glasses off a shelf stacked with more plates, all emblazoned with state flags. She blew into the glasses to remove some of the cat hair. "Let's get started," she said, and raised her eyebrows.

I twisted off the cap and filled her glass almost to the rim, then did the same to mine.

"God, we'll both end up passed out, and forget all the nasty business we were going to catch up on." Then she grinned and made a series of kissing noises.

I took a big sip and hoped I passed out first.

"So," she said over our eggplant dish. "What finally brought you to your senses?"

We were seated at her kitchen table. The gray-striped cat had disappeared, and now a black one nestled on Brenda's lap. She occasionally pinched a bit of food between her thumb and forefinger, and attempted to feed the cat who clearly wanted nothing to do with eggplant. Throughout the course of the meal, the cat continued to never show any interest and Brenda would ultimately stick the morsel into her mouth.

Actually, the eggplant dish was pretty good and I was on a second helping. Either the wine, the Benadryl, or both were kicking in, and I was beginning to experience some difficulty focusing on our conversation. Plus, I was trying to avoid putting my foot in the cat litter box sitting beneath the kitchen table. I'd already kicked it at least a half dozen times spilling some of the contents onto the floor. Brenda was beginning to slur her words, apparently oblivious to the cat litter I'd scattered over her feet.

"Hit me again, Devil," she giggled, then held out her empty glass. I got to my feet, kicked the litter box in the process, and stumbled to the kitchen counter. Brenda turned in her chair and faced me with a wry smile as she held out her glass. I noticed that her leather vest had become unbuttoned, leaving her rather exposed, not a complaint on my part. Somewhere over the course of feasting on eggplant, the black cat had vanished and I think Princess Di was now on her lap.

I attempted to fill her wine glass, but my hand kept weaving from side to side missing the glass occasionally and spilling wine across her thighs. I stopped once her glass was half full.

"Don't hold back, I want it all," she grinned, then bit her lower lip seductively and let out a loud "Meow."

By the time I had finished filling her glass, there were four or five cats in the room swirling around her feet. She noisily slurped her wine, then leered at me, and growled in a deep voice, "They like to watch."

'Great', I thought, a third personality and I dug into my pocket to take two more Benadryl.

It was sometime after three in the morning, Brenda was snoring, wearing her garter belt and one stocking. There were at least three cats in the bed with us. I climbed out of bed and made my way to the bathroom in the dark. There were stacks of collectable stuff piled all over the bedroom and I had to negotiate the narrow, cleared path leading to the bathroom. I think it was a cat that ran into the bedroom as I opened the door. I closed the bathroom door and turned on the light. My face was red and blotchy. My eyes were swollen, and I looked like I'd gone a round with Mike Tyson. I was unable to breath through my nose, and I'd broken out in what looked like hives on my neck, arms, and chest. I remained in the bathroom for a good half hour hoping my sinuses would clear. They didn't and I finally turned out the light, and headed back into Brenda's bedroom.

At first I thought she was up, but then in the moonlight coming through the open basement window I saw her in bed and heard her snoring. A large figure seemed to drift quietly across the narrow path, even in heels Brenda wasn't six feet tall, plus she didn't have a shaved head. He seemed to stare at her, well and the cats, probably wondering what in the hell was going on.

He pulled his T-shirt over his head then cautiously unbuckled his jeans. A cat circled my ankles. I think it was Princess Di, but couldn't be sure in the dark. I quickly picked it up, then whispered, "Excuse me."

As he turned, I tossed the cat toward his face. It sailed screeching through the air, flaying with its paws, as it flew across the room, claws out looking for anything to clamp onto. The sides of his face turned out to be most convenient.

Princess Di clamped on just above his ears and hung on for dear life. He screamed, then attempted to pull her off, which only made her dig those claws in deeper. It gave me the opportunity to aim a well placed kick that dropped him to his knees. As he landed on the floor, Princess Di released her grip, and scampered under the bed. I picked up an empty wine bottle and hit him over the head. It gave off a hollow sort of 'thunk' sound, so I hit him again, and he stopped moving.

I didn't recognize the guy, and wasn't about to take the time to ask any questions. Brenda half groaned, rolled over on her side, and resumed snoring as two cats snuggled up against her.

I looked for my clothes and quickly got dressed, then called 911 from Brenda's phone in the living room, and reported a burglary in progress. I slipped out the door and into my car. As I rounded the corner, I saw flashing lights about three blocks back racing down the street.

Chapter Twenty-Six

It was the knock on the driver's side window that woke me.

"You look like absolute shit," Charlie Bergstrom said as I stepped out of the Aztek. "What are doing up here again, anyway."

I had to lick some of last nights wine off my teeth, and spit another cat hair from my lips, before I could speak. At least the swelling around my eyes had gone down, and I could almost breathe through my nose again. My arms still had welts from the hives, but not as severe as last night, and the constant itching had pretty much subsided. "Just in the neighborhood, thought I'd drop in and say hi."

Charlie just shook his head and said, "Come on in and I'll make you breakfast, you can maybe get cleaned up, a shower is definitely in order."

I was feeling a thousand percent better after the shower. We were sitting out on Charlie's deck, eating pancakes and drinking coffee. I was dressed in a clean shirt and a pair of Daryl's jeans.

"So, she's with the old man, Tubby, and not that jackass son of his," Charlie said, and then sipped some coffee.

"Looks that way. To tell you the truth, no one is more surprised than me. I sort of knew her in a different life. But, there they were, the two of them. She was sitting on his lap and nibbling his ear while old Tubby was working his way through a very large pizza."

"And then those guys got you."

"Yeah, my fault for not paying better attention."

Charlie nodded, like that was a given. "Think they would have killed you?"

"No 'think' about it. That was they're plan. They as much as said so, something about 'now it was going to be a late night' because they had to deal with me. I'm a hundred-percent sure on what 'deal with me' meant. Not pretty."

"So you're back here like a bad check."

"I suppose, I honestly don't know where else to go. I'm willing to bet they got folks in jail, just waiting. Most likely, people ready to track me on the street. I'm sure they're watching my house, my office, and any friend's place, just waiting to nail me. I made it out last night, but my luck can't keep working like this, sooner or later it's gonna run out, it has to, the law of something or other. Whoever that guy was last night, how in the hell did he even find me? I don't know…"

"You ever think about going to the police?"

"You sound like my office pal, Louie. Based on your son's experience, that may be the worst place I could end up."

He nodded, but didn't say anything for a while. "Are they on the take down there in the cities, the cops?"

"No, I don't think so. I think they're sort of caught between a rock and a hard place. They can't really do much until an actual crime has been committed. The problem is the *crime* they seem to want to commit is to kill me."

"From everything you've told me, I think it's probably past the time when you can just sit back and attempt to hide from reality. Might be time to get a little more aggressive."

"Aggressive? You mean like start killing these guys, or going after Tubby, good luck there."

"Well, I think all of this, everything you've told me, still seems to revolve around that drug shipment, the cocaine. Get back to basics, that's where the emphasis should be. All the rest of this nonsense is just a distraction, a side show."

"I'm not sure I want to go there," I said.

"I'm pretty sure until you do, this sort of thing is going to continue. Find where that stuff is stashed, and get it back in DEA custody. You do that, and your pal, Tubby and his crew, will have a lot more on their plate than worrying about you. When was that stuff highjacked from the DEA, a few days ago? I'll lay you odds, they still got it wrapped up somewhere waiting for things to cool down, so they can move it. That's your ticket. You find that shipment and you'll be safe."

Chapter Twenty-Seven

On my way back into town from Daryl Bergstrom's, I was thinking of all the property I'd seen listed to Big Boy Enterprises on the internet. Not the office buildings, restaurants, or bars, but the low-rent dives listed as 'restoration works in progress', like the place where Destiny Meyers was murdered. A place like that might be the perfect locale to hide a highjacked van full of contraband. Well, as long as you could keep the residents away.

I pulled into an internet café on the East side of town. I think I was the only native English speaker in the place. I paid cash for an hour online, and sat in a cigarette-stained, Formica booth, next to an overflowing ashtray, and three empty Starbuck's cups, searching the Big Boy Enterprises website.

There were seven *'work in progress'* addresses listed on the web site. I drove past all of them in the early afternoon, then drove back to the one where Destiny Meyers and Duncan Nixon had camped out. Nothing had improved over the ensuing week. The security system on the front door was still deactivated, so I just walked in. The hallway leading back to Destiny's former nest was littered with a mattress, empty, half-pint liquor bottles, and a condom. The door on the room next to hers was still open, but there was a different guy passed out on the floor.

I wandered through the first floor, and after opening two closet doors, found an entrance leading to the basement. The last time I'd been in a basement, someone was squeezing my hand in a vice, and planning to kill me, so I descended with some trepidation. Oddly the light switch worked.

As I descended the staircase, the smell from moldy fabric grew substantially stronger. Three quarters of the way down, I halted on the stairs, and surveyed the mess. Along with a furnace, two discarded water heaters, and a third functioning unit, the basement held some useless bicycles, a card table with three legs, and a kennel cage for a small dog. The room was cool, very damp, and the entire floor was covered with moldy items of clothing. There was a mound around the base of the staircase that suggested people had simply taken a few steps down and then tossed whatever they were carrying into the basement making the item no longer their problem. Nowhere was there anything that resembled two pallets of cocaine bricks.

The unlocked, three-stall garage held a menagerie of broken and discarded chairs, tables, beds, a stack of kitchen cabinets, and a cracked granite counter top. Ladders and tools sporting a variety of contactor's names were stacked haphazardly against a far wall. Six very used looking car batteries were piled next to the door.

The next three addresses were pretty much the same, although one of them did have a locked front door. The fourth place was slightly different. Fortunately, or unfortunately depending on your view, the back door was not only open, it had been torn off its hinges, and leaned against the wall in a small hallway. I walked in and entered what had probably been a fairly decent kitchen back in about 1960. The worn enamel sink was full of dishes and pots that had obviously been there for awhile. Three cigarette butts rested in, what at one point may have been a plate of macaroni and cheese.

I debated going through the next door when it opened, and what used to be a woman floated into the room.

When she spoke I could see a good portion of her teeth were either missing or just jagged remnants in her mouth. Her cheeks were sunken and she was so thin and pale that any semblance of a figure had long ago disappeared. She was ghostlike. We were a good five feet apart, but I could smell her, and it wasn't pleasant.

"Got a cigarette?" she half whispered, then brushed a wisp of thinning hair off her forehead.

"No sorry, I was looking for the basement," I said.

She gave me a strange look, shrugged like she didn't know what I was talking about or didn't care, and drifted back from where she'd come leaving the door open.

I followed her and said, "I need to get into your garage."

She sat down on a torn couch, propped up with two bricks at one end. The couch was littered with clothes and a couple of dirty paper plates. She just stared at me.

"Your garage, you got a key to get in there."

"Benny said he didn't want anyone going in there."

"Yeah, I know, but he told me to get something for him. I just need to get in there and grab it, then I'll leave. I could make it worth your while," I said and pulled out a couple of bucks from my pocket. I moved my hand holding the bills back and forth a few times and she followed the cash with her eyes like a dog following a bone. Eventually, she said, "Okay," and held out her hand.

"You can get me in there?"

"I can tell you how, but you gotta appreciate me first," she said and stared at the bills.

I handed her the cash. She quickly stuffed it in her pocket as she stood, then walked to a door on the far side of the room. I thought she might be going for a key, when she stopped and turned.

"You just knock on the door and one of Benny's pals will let you in. There's always someone in there. 'Course you'd know that already seeing as how Benny was the one sent you over here to get something," she said, then gave me a brief glance before she floated out the door.

If Tubby's kid Ben or one of his friends was locked in the garage I suspected it wasn't because they were changing the oil on a car. I wondered if they had seen me come in the back door. I decided it might make sense to find the front exit to this dive. I followed her path out the door and into another trash littered hallway, but the ghost was nowhere to be seen.

Chapter Twenty-Eight

The last thing I needed was some whacko like Bulldog recognizing my car, so I pulled it down the street, then walked back and hid behind a hedge surrounding the backyard next door. For the longest time the only activity was me slapping mosquitoes.

Just about dusk, some fat guy with spiked hair wearing a black T-shirt and blue jeans walked up the driveway, and knocked on the garage door. A sort of muffled voice I couldn't understand called out something from inside.

"It's Jace, open the door, dumb-shit," the fat guy said.

A moment later the side door opened and he stepped in. About fifteen minutes after that a different figure in camouflaged shorts, wearing a Jim Beam T-shirt, stepped out of the garage, and hurried down the driveway talking on his cellphone. "Hey, calm down. I said, I'll be there in fifteen minutes, so quit bitching." He had traveled too far down the driveway to pick up any more of his conversation, but it sounded like it wasn't going to be a very fun night.

I sat in the hedge getting eaten alive by mosquitoes for another couple of hours, but nothing happened. I ultimately tired of waiting, cautiously approached the garage, and knocked on the door.

A voice responded from inside, but I couldn't make out exactly what he said.

"It's me, dumb-shit. Open up, I forgot something," I said, then crouched ready to either spring inside or run for cover.

There was a long pause, and then the voice said "Bobby?" or "Robby?" I couldn't be sure which.

"Come on, Jace. I'm getting eaten alive out here by these damn mosquitoes. Open the door, damn it."

The door opened a moment later as a voice said, "You're supposed to text me before you…"

I hit him hard between the eyes just as he began to focus on me. He didn't go down, instead he staggered back a step or two. I gave him a sharp crack to the throat, and he clutched reflexively with both hands, dropping a pistol in the process. I kicked him hard in the knee, and heard a crack as he went down. He was rolling on the floor crying, as I picked up his pistol. "Nice to meet you, Jace."

A flat screen TV sat on top of an olive drab file cabinet. It was tuned to what looked like professional wrestling. There were two dark green plastic chairs and a card table in front of the flat screen. An open pizza box and a can of beer rested on the card table. I helped myself to a slice of pizza.

Jace had stopped rolling, but was still on the floor only now he was just grunting and watching me eat his pizza.

"Mmm-mmm, pretty good, only I've always liked black olives on mine. So, Jace," I said looking around. "Just what in the hell are you doing here?"

It was a standard two stall garage from about 1960 with a large oil stain on the floor of the nearest stall.

There were some rakes and a snow shovel hanging on the back wall, and a rusty-black Ford Ranger pickup in the furthest stall. The truck had been backed in, and there was a blue tarp, covering whatever was stacked in the bed of the pickup. The tarp was tied down with a braided yellow cord. I kept my eye on Jace, as I walked over to the tarp, untied the cord and lifted a corner.

There, packaged in what looked like Saran Wrap and duct tape, neatly stacked, were a number of white powder bricks. I pulled the tarp back further to reveal more bricks all perfectly arraigned.

"You got any idea who you're fucking with?" Jace gasped then groaned. He was still rolling from side to side and there was a fine coating of dust on his jeans and T-shirt from the garage floor. His nose was bleeding, and had formed a sort of bloody goatee dripping down to his chin.

I just smiled at him, pulled out my cell, and dialed a number.

"You don't have any idea the trouble you're in, they'll kill you for this. Believe me, I ain't kidding, pal, your ass is as good as dead," Jace groaned from the floor.

"I'm sort of busy right now, can it wait?" Aaron LaZelle said, on the other end of the line. I could hear music and some other voices in the background, sounding like a bar or maybe a restaurant.

"Not if you want to get that hijacked DEA stash back in your possession."

There was a long pause before he spoke. "You better not be joking."

Jace was still on the floor, but he was shaking his head, and suddenly looking very worried.

"Believe me, I'm not joking. You got a color crayon and a clean spot on the wall so you can write down this address? It's over on the East side."

"Go ahead."

I gave him the address then said, "It's in the garage, there's one unarmed individual rolling around on the floor of the garage wearing dirty blue jeans and a black T-shirt. I don't intend to be here when your people arrive. But, I wouldn't waste any time if I were you."

"You're going to need protection," Aaron said.

"I don't think you can give it right now," I said and hung up.

"You are so God damned stupid. You don't know what in the hell you've done. They're going to kill you, probably kill both of us."

"Then we better get out of here, both of us, before the police arrive."

He looked at me strangely.

"Can you walk? See if you can stand."

He stared at me for a moment like he didn't believe me, then hobbled and half climbed to his feet. He took half a step then collapsed into one of the plastic chairs. "Ahh-hhh, Jesus that hurts. I can't, man it hurts too damn much."

"You got a car here?"

"Parked across the street."

"Give me your keys, I'll get it for you."

He glanced at me for a moment like he didn't believe me, then slowly pulled a set of keys out of his jeans and set them on the table.

"Maybe toss them over here to me."

He tossed the keys to me, but in an easy way so I could catch them. "It's that black paneled van out there, couple doors down." He nodded his head to indicate the direction.

"I'll get it. See if you can make it to the door," I said then hurried out.

The paneled van looked like a late 90's model, and reeked of cigarette smoke. I got in behind the wheel and started it up. Then, just to play it safe, I opened the glove compartment. There was a small revolver that looked like a .38 snub in there under a couple of road maps. It held five shells and I stuffed them in my pocket, then returned the weapon to where I'd found it. I pulled the van down the street then backed up the driveway, as I rolled closer to the garage fat, dusty Jace jiggled up against the door frame.

I left the engine on and the door open then said, "If I were you I'd get the hell out of here. You can't have more than a couple of minutes before the cops are here."

He nodded and hobbled his way toward the driver's door using the side of the van for support. I watched as he groaned and gingerly dragged his leg into the van, then I walked down the driveway. I was almost to my car when the van finally pulled out of the driveway and then came along side of me. As I glanced over, the passenger window came down. Jace flashed a wide grin as he held his cellphone in his left hand ready to take a picture. "Little something extra for you, asshole," he said, then aimed the snub .38 revolver at me with his right hand and pulled the trigger.

'Click.'

He pulled the trigger twice more with the same result then shouted, "God damn it."

I reached in and yanked the pistol out of his hand just before he raced off. I hurried over to the Aztek and took off in the opposite direction.

Chapter Twenty-Nine

The headline in the morning paper was something about a city-wide recycling effort being put on hold due to funding shortfalls. The local radio and television news mentioned the latest grim news from the Mideast, and then spent a substantial amount of time on the wedding of a reality 'star' I'd never heard of. I couldn't find anything about the cocaine bust online, although I was attempting to look via my cellphone and not having much success. Aaron LaZelle wasn't answering my calls. After sleeping in my car, I'd spent the better part of the morning in a truck stop diner about fifteen miles outside of town on Interstate 35, eating giant blueberry pancakes, apple bacon and drinking very strong coffee.

I figured the first thing I had to do was get rid of the Aztek. Not that that would really bother me, I hated the thing anyway. I placed a call to my sometime auto source, Walter, and like usual left a message. He called me back about fifteen minutes later.

"Hello."

"Where you at?"

"Walter?"

"Returning your call. Not sure where you're sitting right now, only know it ain't far enough away from here."

"Hunh?"

"You got some nasty folks looking for your ass, Dev. Wherever you are, you best keep going."

"That's part of my problem, there's some not nice people in town looking for my car. They already spotted it once, I need a different set of wheels."

"What you need is a plane ticket to somewhere very far away."

"You kidding, they're probably watching the airport. Can you help me, Walter? You're one of the few people I can trust right now."

"Humpf. Now that's something I don't hear very often. Lucky for you I'm not too fond of the gentleman that's lookin' to burn your ass."

"How'd you hear about it? It wasn't on the news or online."

"Online, shit. You kidding me, probably no more than a half hour after you made that bust and everyone heard, Dev. Words out on the street 'bout you. Your man says he'll pay nicely to get his hands on you."

"Tubby?"

"Mmm-hmm."

"So can you help me?"

"I can, but like always it's going to cost you for my time."

"Cost me, like what are we talking a couple three grand?"

"You should be so lucky, maybe triple that."

"You gotta be kiddin me, seven?"

"More like ten, Dev."

"Ten?"

"Look, I'm taking an awfully big chance. I don't like the man, but I don't need no trouble with the son-of-a-bitch either. You hear?"

"If I can scrounge up the cash when can I get this?"

"Soon as you get the cash, I got just the thing for you. Only I don't want you coming anywhere near here. You get that cash, you let me know where you at, I'll send someone. Don't want your ass around here, you're bad for business right now."

"Can I get some trade in value on what I'm driving? It's a real great Aztek and..."

"No it ain't, and it's got no value, zero, you hear? That thing is associated with you so it ain't worth shit."

"You sure? See I was thinking that if you maybe repainted and..."

"You heard my offer, and I'm going out on a limb making it, so either take it or leave it. Let me know today. Good-bye," he said and hung up.

I phoned Louie, amazingly he answered.

"Dev?"

"Yeah, you in the office?"

"No, actually I'm heading into court. About to attempt to plead down a second DWI for some numbskull who..."

"Louie, Louie hold on, just listen. Okay? I need ten grand, fast."

"Ten, are you kidding. Where are you going to get..."

"Louie, I got three in the back of my desk, bottom drawer, the one with all the files, it's in an envelope taped to the bottom side of the drawer."

"You're kidding me. Really?"

"Yeah. Then, take one of my business checks, write a check to you for four grand and cash it."

"Okay. I can do that, I guess."

"Then do you think you could loan me three? I'm good for it."

"What the hell did you do?"

"Let's just say I tried to do the right thing and leave it at that."

"You okay, Dev?"

"So far. Look I need you to go to the Trend Bar, you know the place?"

"That joint on University?"

"Yeah, give the cash to a guy named Walter, he's always at the end of the bar. He'll be dressed in some fancy suit, drinking coffee, maybe talking to someone. Just ask to speak with him. I'll let him know you're coming."

"Dev, I'm ready to step into the courtroom now, it'll be a while before I can do all this."

"Just let me know when you're on your way. I'm counting on you, Louie, you're my only hope."

"Jesus, Dev just go to the damn cops, will you?"

"I did, sort of, I think that's why the heats on."

"God, Dev. Okay, I'll do it, but it's gonna take a little time."

"Just call me when you're on the way to see Walter, and Louie, watch out for tails. Some jerk may be watching you."

"Great. Thanks for that."

Chapter Thirty

I waited in the truck stop parking lot through most of the hot, muggy afternoon. I watched about a thousand folks gas up their cars, maybe two thousand folks use the rest rooms, and I saw a little girl and a dog throw up. A Minnesota Highway Patrol car cruised past twice and gave me the eye. The second time he passed by very slowly. I figured if he came round again he was going to stop and ask me if *'everything is okay'*. It was a little after three when Louie called me back.

"Louie," I answered as soon as I saw his number.

"Dev, sorry for the delay. Your bank sort of gave me a hassle."

"That check for four grand should be good, I think."

"Yeah, it was, but the teller brought it to some junior officer. He took one look at me and brought it over to his boss. I finally got the cash, but it took them awhile."

"You heading toward Walter?"

"That guy at The Trend?"

"Yeah."

"I should be there in the next fifteen minutes. Look, Dev, I don't know what's going on, but take some advice from your lawyer, here. Turn yourself in."

"Remember what happened to Daryl Bergstrom?"

"You mean that kid who was murdered while in jail?"

"Yeah. Then the guy that killed him, Duncan Nixon."

"Mmm-mmm."

"I'm thinking even if they put me in protective custody, Tubby could find a way to get to me."

"So where are you going?"

"The only place I can, I'm going after Tubby."

"What the..."

"I'll call Walter and let him know you're on the way. Then watch your back, Louie. Tubby's got a lot of folks looking for me, and he's bound to have someone keeping an eye on you."

"Hold on, think about this, Dev."

"I have, Louie, and I'm out of options. They're bound to find me wherever I try and hide."

"God, just take care of yourself, man."

"You just get that dough over to Walter, and thanks, I couldn't do this without you."

"I'm not sure that makes me feel very good."

"I'll call Walter," I said, and hung up.

Walter wasn't taking any chances, which is probably why he's lasted this long, and been so successful. He asked where I was, then told me he'd call back as soon as he was paid with the location where my new car would be.

I found the car in an outdated mall parking lot, parked in front of a liquor store advertising 10% off all half pints. It was tough to miss, a Honda Integra sporting California plates, and missing the better part of its front grill. The thing was a faded powder blue, with the exception of the trunk which was a faded pink. A crack about four inches above the dash ran across the front windshield. There was a gaping hole where the passenger side mirror had been torn off and the door was buckled. A sticker on the rear bumper read *'Grow your own dope, plant a man.'*

The key ring was under the driver's side floor mat, and sported a Palm Beach Feline Rescue logo. I flashed back to my ill-conceived evening with Brenda Livingston, and immediately began to itch. As I slid into the driver's seat I noticed that the radio had been ripped out of the dash. At least the car started.

I'll give it this much, it seemed to have speed, but then again I was comparing it to the Aztec which wasn't much of a challenge. I drove back into town, then sat in the middle of an empty high school parking lot for the next few hours, constantly looking around in all directions. Once the sun went down, I drove over to Crickett's house and parked up the street.

Sure enough, a little before midnight, two sets of headlights drifted down the street. Just like before, a shiny black car pulled to the curb while the second vehicle, an SUV of some sort remained in the street. The door opened on the first car, and a guy climbed out. Only this time it wasn't Tubby, but what looked like a substantially thinner version of him. Tubby's kid Ben?

Crickett held the door open for him as he trotted up the steps then slipped inside, she closed the door behind her and turned out the front porch light. A moment later the front drapes were pulled closed, and the second car drove down the street past me just as I ducked down behind the wheel.

I knew better than to window peek at the back of the house. Instead, I played it safe and took a round about route through the neighborhood, checking for the SUV. I didn't see anything resembling the thing, so I parked a block over, then cautiously walked up the alley. I didn't meet anyone.

I was thinking of maybe waiting in the back seat of the *'BeniBoy'* Mercedes, but it was locked. Plus, I figured there might be a good chance he wouldn't exit the house until his escort vehicle had been summoned. I crawled back in the Integra up on the next block and waited. I dosed off at some point and woke to the sound of a distant car door slamming. It wasn't quite 6:00am.

As I blinked awake, I saw the Mercedes pull away from the curb, with the black SUV following right behind. I could just barely make out two silhouettes in the front seat of the SUV. With almost no traffic on the streets, I followed cautiously hanging back almost two blocks. Both vehicles entered the underground parking ramp of a trendy condo building along the river bluff. I pulled around the corner, and then checked the list I'd made of properties owned by Big Boy Enterprises. Sure enough the building was listed. It was a far cry from the *'restoration in progress'* dives I'd been through the other day.

This building was ten floors of palatial million-dollar units, and it was a pretty safe guess, Tubby's kid lived in one of them. I'd been in the building once before, some sort of wedding or funeral thing, I couldn't quite recall. I did recall that it had a security system, and you had to dial a tenant from the lobby. There were security cameras in the entryway, the lobby, and the elevators. I figured there had to be a better way to spend my time.

Chapter Thirty-One

After ringing the door bell repeatedly, I started pounding until Crickett finally answered looking shocked to see me. She gave me this wide eyed sort of grimacing gasp when she opened the door, like someone she knew was just about to jump off a cliff.

"Hi, Crickett, mind if I come in?" I said then half-shouldered the door and pushed past her before she could slam it shut. She was dressed in another robe, but apparently she'd come up in the world since this one was an exotic looking black and red silk kimono with lapels, instead of the raunchy blue terricloth rag from her distant past. The kimono covered barely an inch of her thighs, with a sexy slit on the sides that rose above her inviting hips.

I, on the other hand, had slept in my car last night and was wearing the same clothes I'd sweated in for the last two days. I hadn't showered for over forty-eight hours of hot, muggy weather, and I was still coughing up the occasional cat hair. I held the snub .38 in my front pocket.

"You just better leave, Dev, if you know what's good for you. Certain very important people won't be too happy to learn you're here."

"Then maybe it wouldn't be a good idea to tell them, now would it?"

"I don't think you quite understand…"

"Oh, I understand, honey, believe me, I'm understanding a little bit more with every passing hour. How's Tubby by the way? It must be exhausting doing a father and son at the same time."

"I wouldn't have the slightest idea what in the hell you're talking about," she said, but the flushed face and the edgy tone of her denial suggested a much different story.

"Drop the act, Crickett, or should I just go back to calling you Karen? I saw you in here the other night gnawing on Tubby's ear while he inhaled a giant pizza. I hope for your sake you get to take tops, I wouldn't want him rolling over on me. Of course you were back riding 'BeniBoy' last night. God, such a busy girl you're making it tough for me to keep up, sweetie."

"They're never going to stop looking for you after what you did to Ricky and Eddie the other night."

"Ricky and Eddie? Are they the two thugs that had my hand in the vice down in your basement? The two guys pissed off because they were going to have to waste their night killing me and hiding the body? Those two fools? You're lucky I didn't come after you, bitch."

The color drained from her face as she pulled the kimono tighter around her waist and stared at her feet. When she looked up she was a changed woman. She gave me that half smile and wide eyed stare that used to make me flop over on my back, and pant like a dog.

"It's just that once you dumped me, Dev, I sort of went crazy. I've never been able to find the man who could completely replace you. Honest, I've been looking. You know I'd do anything, and I mean anything to get you back," she said, then let the Kimono fall open as she took half a step toward me. "Anything," she half whispered.

"You mean like have me killed. They were going to kill me, Crickett." I spit out her name.

She pulled the kimono tight around her waist again, like a bedroom door slamming in my face. "Oh get over it, you're here to tell the story."

"Here to tell the story? I wouldn't even be here, wouldn't be involved, God there wouldn't even be a story if you hadn't asked me to help you. The whole thing has been a set up right from the start. Why did you ever contact me? Why did you ask for my help with Daryl?"

"That loser? Spare me."

"Spare me? The guy is dead because of you. You basically set him up just as much as your psycho lovers, Ben and Tubby. Hell, is that kid, the little baby even..."

"His name is Oliver."

"Is Oliver even his, Daryl's?"

"Yeah, well at least I think so. He probably is," she said, then wrinkled her nose like she wasn't all that sure.

"God. The guy was murdered waiting to make a plea bargain on a deal that was a setup right from the start. You were part of that, you helped set him up, and you might just as well have been the one who slit his throat."

"I set him up? Where do you get that? I didn't ask him to drive that van. I didn't give him a hundred bucks. Don't you think it's just a little strange someone asks you to drive a van into a parking lot, and as an adult you don't ask any questions?"

"Strange? Yeah, especially when you add the fact that your so-called girlfriend is sleeping with the guy making the offer, and his lunatic father. Maybe he wanted to get on your good side. Maybe he wanted to show you he was as good as your lowlife fuck-buddy Ben. Maybe he wanted to get you back. Maybe he didn't want to lose the baby. I don't know, maybe he was just plain stupid, which would explain a lot, starting with ending up with you. Jesus, Karen..."

"It's Crickett!"

"God, you're ten years older than he is. What the hell, maybe he just had a mother infatuation."

She took a swing at me, but I blocked it.

"Get out of here, get out of my home, now."

"Your home? You don't own this place. Daryl's father, Charlie owns it. You're going to be out in the street, *Crickett*. You think the father and son Gustafson gang you've been tag teaming is going to take you in. They'll have you dancing in one of Tubby's strip bars for tips and snorts of cocaine."

"They love me, and if I were you I'd be packing to go far away. Very far away, they aren't going to rest until they get you, Dev. That's not a warning, that's a promise. You screwed up everything and they won't forget."

"You better think about it, Crickett, because you screwed up everything when you got me involved. You let them know I'm coming after them. I'm going to get Ben and Tubby and then you and nothing, not even that wacko psychopath Bulldog, is going to stop me."

Her chest heaved, and I could hear her breathing heavily through her nose, like she'd just run a dash and lost. Maybe that was it, she realized regardless of what happened, she was going to lose. Probably sooner rather than later, both Tubby and Ben would grow tired of her. Charlie Bergstrom was going to kick her out on the street, and then my prediction about dancing for tips and snorts of cocaine wasn't that far from the truth.

143

"Get out of here, get out of my house. I'm calling them right now," she said. Her voice was cold, devoid of emotion, she strutted over to the coffee table, and made a show of picking up a cellphone, managing to expose herself in the process.

"That would probably be a good idea, Crickett. But while you're talking to them, remember you're on borrowed time. No matter how sexy you think you are, no matter how clever you think you are playing one off the other, sooner or later they'll have had enough of your shit, and then *you* better start packing. When they answer, you tell them I'm on my way."

She made a show of pushing a speed dial number, crossed her arms over her chest then gave me a look that suggested *'I'll show you'*. She put the cell to her ear and stared. I decided it might be a good time to make fast tracks out the front door. I left the door open as my own departing gesture, then heard it slam behind me before I was off her front steps. The boom made me half jump, and I picked up speed heading to my car.

Chapter Thirty-Two

After making my big play with Crickett, I fled the scene as fast as possible with no idea where I could go. The Spot was out, same thing with Louie's, Heidi's, my office, not to mention my house. Just thinking about Brenda's cats made me itch, and my nose started to run, besides someone had spotted my car there, and they were still probably watching the place. I headed back to Ben's trendy condo building, and parked in the visitor's space in the next building over.

Ben's condo was just off Shepard Road, overlooking the Mississippi. There was a tugboat out there pushing six barges down river, probably heading to St. Louis, or maybe all the way down to New Orleans. For a half second I thought about trying to swim out to the thing, and just floating my way out of town. Instead, I grabbed a push broom from a side patio area, and made my way to the underground parking entrance.

I swept back and forth across the entrance for the better part of a half hour, then gave a friendly wave like an employee might do when the door finally opened, and some bald guy in a BMW zipped out of the parking area and up the ramp. He ignored me, didn't give me so much as the finger which was just fine with me. I quickly swept my way into the parking garage just before the door closed.

It was a large, mostly empty parking area at this hour of the day. I recognized the black Mercedes with the *'BeniBoy'* plates, and the black SUV parked next to it in the two spaces closet to the elevator. The spaces were numbered with what I guessed were unit numbers, 1001 and 1002. It figured, in a condo building with ten floors of course Tubby's kid would want to be on the top floor, above everyone else, and then grab the two parking spaces closest to the elevator.

I guessed that if the two vehicles were still here, apparently Crickett hadn't gotten around to actually making her phone call. Her picking up the cellphone and making a big scene had probably all been an act. Unless she'd called Tubby, but then it seemed likely that Tubby would have dispatched Ben and his two minders so he could remain at the food trough.

I wasn't sure what to do. I thought about letting the air out of their tires, but noticed the security cameras mounted on the walls. On the off chance they were monitored some nitwit might be watching me, wondering what in the hell I was doing. I rested the broom next to the garage door, then walked over and pushed the 'up' button for the elevator. The doors opened a second later.

I stepped in and noticed another security camera, this one with a blinking green light. I pushed the button for the tenth floor. My ride up was uninterrupted, and all too fast. What sounded like a church bell clanged to announce my arrival. The doors opened onto a hallway with plush, floral pattern carpet on a navy blue background. Dark paneling ran up the wall to about shoulder height. I stepped out of the elevator and glanced around. My hand was tightly wrapped around the snub .38 in my pocket. It looked like there were only two units on the tenth floor, 1001 and 1002.

I figured since he was Tubby's kid, Ben would naturally want to be first, so I knocked softly on the door labeled 1001 and waited. The door opened a moment later, and even with the surprised look on his face as I pushed the .38 against his nose, I could see the resemblance to Tubby. He had the beginning of a ruddy complexion on his full face, and a pair of ears that would continue to grow for the next thirty years. Add a bulbous nose, three or four more chins, maybe another three hundred pounds, with some food smeared around his mouth, and it was Tubby.

A .38 pressed against the nose is an impressive way of getting an individual to back up. Ben cautiously stepped back into a large living room with a dark wood floor. He was in stocking feet and kept his hands raised in surrender. His eyes almost crossed, as he continued to focus on the barrel of the .38.

"You're that Dev Haskell guy."

"Anyone else in here?"

He shook his head no.

"And you're Tubby's son, Ben. That right?"

He nodded.

"Back up a little bit more and keep those hands up. You carrying, Ben? You got a weapon on you?"

"No sir. And no one else is in here."

"I hope you're not lying, because no matter what they do, I'll have the half second on my side that it'll take me to shoot you right between the eyes."

"Honest, Mr. Haskell no one is in here, except for you and me."

"What about your neighbors across the hall in 1002?"

"Who?" he asked trying to play dumb.

"Ben, don't screw with me, two guys, thick necks, ride around town in a black SUV, that right now is parked next to your Mercedes."

I caught the sudden flare in the pupils of his eyes. Like he'd made a mistake, and underestimated how much I might know. I decided to push a little further. "Ben, understand something here. You don't tell me the truth, try to bullshit me, I'll know and then you'll never, ever see that little love pal of yours, Cricket, in her sexy little black and red kimono again. Understand?"

His eyes widened even more and he nodded.

"Tell me about the cocaine hijacked from the DEA, Ben."

"I don't know what..." But he stopped in mid-sentence and shook his head. "I can't my dad will kill me."

"Probably, but that's really not my problem. Did you set Daryl Bergstrom up?"

"No, honest. Daryl knew, or well we both knew the van was being watched. But it was his idea, he figured it was worth the chance and he'd be able to just talk his way out of it if the cops actually caught him. He was thinking it would be a joy ride, an adventure sort of deal. He didn't even know they were tailing him. Suddenly, everything just really backfired, and the cops were all over him. Then some lunatic killed him while he was in jail."

"Duncan Nixon."

"Yeah, but my dad took care of him."

He made it sound like he had no idea Tubby was the one responsible for Nixon killing Daryl in the first place.

"Who's score was it, the cocaine."

"I don't know, honest. Daryl said he heard about it, but I never knew who told him. He figured if we could get it in police custody, it was large enough that the DEA would have to get involved. Then he figured the vulnerable point would be when they transferred custody to the DEA. So when you gave my dad that information we were all set. If there's a payment problem or something between you and my dad, you should probably be talking to him. I'm really not involved with that sort of…"

"A payment problem. That's what you think this is all about? A payment problem?"

"Well, yeah, I guess."

"You guess? Ben, you got a number of very dead people, and that number just might continue to grow," I said, and shoved the .38 in his direction making him flinch. "Here's the deal, my friend, I want my life back. I don't want you, your old man, or that piece of shit Bulldog after me. I don't want any payment. I don't have anything you want or need. The cocaine, which you say never really belonged to you in the first place, is back in police or DEA custody. Maybe you can come up with a way to get hold of it again, maybe not. Not my concern. I just want to be left alone. Got it?"

He looked somewhat quizzically at me, but nodded.

"Say it," I said, and thrust the .38 toward his head.

"Yes, sir. I get it. You just want to be left alone."

"That's right, and if I'm not. If someone comes after me, I have information set to go to the police that will incriminate everyone. You, your old man, Bulldog, and even sexy little Crickett, understand?"

"Yeah, yeah, I mean, yes sir."

"We'll see. Why don't you take that belt off and kneel down on the floor."

He gave me a worried look.

"Just do it. If I wanted to kill you, I wouldn't have wasted my precious time talking to you. Come on, give me the belt and kneel down."

He handed me his belt, knelt down on the floor in front of me, and then started to shake. There were a thousand different things I could think of doing to him right now, but I didn't have the luxury of time.

"Put your arms by your side," I said, then wrapped the belt around his chest and arms and buckled it as tightly as possible in the middle of his back. "Lay face down," I said, and lowered him to the floor holding him by the collar. I pulled off his socks, knotted them together, then tied them around his ankles.

"Just lay there and count to a thousand. I see you out in the hall, or anywhere near my car, I'm going to shoot first and ask questions later. Don't make the mistake of thinking I'm kidding."

"Yes, sir."

"Good boy, Ben. Now, I want you to tell Tubby to back the hell off and leave me alone, or I'm going to come after him, and you, and Crickett. Got it?"

"Yes, sir."

"Don't forget, Ben your life depends on it," I half laughed, then backed out of the door keeping a close eye on Ben. For his part he kept his face glued to the floor, it looked like he's taken my advice to heart. His lips were moving and he seemed to be counting to a thousand.

Chapter Thirty-Three

I hurried onto the elevator, and went down to the parking garage. This time, I took a moment to let the air out of a front tire on both the Mercedes and the SUV then quickly made my way out of the building. I felt like I was being watched as I ran to my car, but no one came after me, and mercifully no one fired a shot.

I placed the .38 in the glove compartment for safe keeping, then backed out of my parking spot. My cell rang just as I was pulling the Integra onto Shepard Road. "Haskell Investigations," I answered, then almost hit a red pickup making an illegal left against the red traffic light. I slammed on the brakes, hit the horn and screeched to a stop.

"Hi, Dev, returning your call," Aaron LaZelle said.

"My call? Jesus, which one, I left about a half dozen." I flicked my middle finger in the direction of the pickup growing ever smaller in my rearview mirror, and turned onto Shepard Road.

"So now I'm calling back. What did you want?"

"Some help for starters, but it's a little late for that."

His voice took on a more serious tone. "Now what did you do?"

"Do? How could I possibly do anything? I got Tubby Gustafson and his thugs looking all over town for me. I can't go home, can't go to my office. Some nut case spotted my car on the street the other night, and broke into an apartment I was staying in. I can't go to you guys because they've no doubt, got some deranged psycho just waiting to slit *my* throat in the shower room."

"Dev, we can give you protection."

"No offense, Aaron, but I think I'm better off looking after myself."

"Oh, yeah, sure, I get it. I mean, it sounds to me like you're really doing a bang-up job."

"Hey, Tubby hasn't been able to get his hands on me, yet."

He didn't respond to that.

"Your guys get that stuff back in custody?"

"Actually there was a bit of a problem with that."

"A problem? What the hell kind of problem?"

"Seems there was a bit of a conflict between our people and the feds."

"Conflict?"

"Yeah, a question of who was going to be in charge."

"But, you got it, right? I mean, tell me someone took the time to go over and get that shit back in custody."

"Seems by the time they finished arguing, then got over there, about all they found were some pizza crusts and an empty garage."

"What? They didn't get the Ford Ranger that was parked there, just waiting for you to pick it up?"

"'Fraid not."

"Oh, God, I don't believe it. You didn't mention my name to those DEA idiots did you?"

"No, you're down as the classic anonymous tip."

"Thanks. What the hell, does the term missed opportunity have any connotation? They sat there and argued with one another while someone else got in there and took the stuff?"

"Yeah, I know. Some heads may eventually roll, not that it helps you any. If it means anything to you, I appreciate the tip, and it's definitely a screw up on this end."

"Thanks, I feel tons better. Jesus." I said, trying to get my head around such a major disaster.

"So, now maybe you'll accept some protection, look you could even come stay with me."

"That's really nice, Aaron. I mean it, but you'd cramp my style. Besides, I'm working on a couple of things, and…"

"Please tell me you're not getting involved with Tubby and his band of misfits."

"No, why in the hell would I do something like that?"

"It just strikes me as something that would be really stupid, and well…"

"Oh yeah, 'really stupid' so therefore I'd do it. Hey, I can honestly say I haven't spoken with Tubby since I don't know when. So just relax."

"Let us help you, Dev. These guys aren't fooling."

"No offense, buddy, but your record is less than sterling. Besides, I've got it under control, Aaron, so dial down, man."

"You're sure?"

"Yup."

"You'll call me if you need anything?"

"I will if you promise to call back?"

"I promise," he said, and we hung up.

I stuffed the cell back in my pocket, still in shock over the fact that they blew their one chance, then glanced in the rearview mirror. The double lane road was empty, with the exception of a vehicle coming up behind me that looked to be in a hurry. I had no idea where I was going, and all day to get there, so I pulled over into the right lane. The vehicle seemed to pick up speed, gaining on me. It figured, just the two of us on the road, and this jerk can sail past forty miles over the speed limit, but I'm the guy who'd get tagged. I watched him in the side mirror as he pulled along side. He seemed to float out there for a brief moment, then just as he was about to pass, he slammed into me, banging off the front wheel on the driver's side.

The Integra bounced, then fishtailed back and forth as I hit the brakes and fought to regain control. My head banged off the side window. I almost had the car back under control, when he bounced off me again and I sailed across the wide shoulder and headed sideways down a grassy incline. I pumped the breaks as I slid down toward a drainage ditch. I felt the car slide sideways and then begin to lift like it might be heading into a roll, but it leveled off and spun around into the drainage ditch. My head banged hard against the window again as the car shuddered to a sudden halt. I waited a moment to catch my breath then attempted to drive forward. I could hear the wheels spinning and not getting any traction. I tried to open the door, but it wouldn't budge. I attempted to shoulder the thing open, but it felt like it was welded shut.

I rolled down the window, angled my way out then dropped into about a foot of mud the consistency of thick pudding. I ended up sitting in there with my arms extended behind me. The mud oozed up above my wrists and over the tops of my shoes. The wheels on the Integra were buried almost to the top of the rims.

"Good things come in shitty packages," a voice growled from behind. I couldn't tell if he was referring to me or the Integra. I tilted my head back and stared upside down at Bulldog holding a very large pistol and flashing a very crooked smile. Two thick necked jerks were side stepping down the incline behind him.

Chapter Thirty-Four

"Get in there and pull his ass out," Bulldog growled then quickly glanced around for anyone watching. It appeared we were all alone.

I heard a car approaching up on Shepard Road, but it sailed past and didn't so much as slow down.

"Keep your damn hands were I can see 'em," he said, as two pairs of beefy paws yanked me effortlessly out of the mud. The mud made a sort of sucking sound as I was pulled out. They kept me at arms length as they dragged me up toward Bulldog.

"This is gonna be fun," Bulldog said, almost jumping up and down in anticipation then he clubbed me on the side of the head with the butt of his pistol. The last thing I remember was he needed a shave, and his teeth were crooked and very yellow.

I was between the seats and down on the cramped floor of some vehicle. I'd been down there for quite a while. I was pretty sure there were two pair of feet resting on me. My head really hurt and some sort of discarded, muddy boot was about a half inch from my face. I kept my eyes closed, and tried to keep my stomach down as we rumbled along a bumpy road. I was afraid if I gave any indication I was conscious they'd start kicking me, so I decided the best policy was to just remain still.

We'd been driving for what seemed like hours, and maybe was, although I really didn't know. As we made a sharp turn, I sort of slid across the floor until my head wedged against the door. Then some giant boot slammed down and held my head in place. The road grew bumpier immediately after the turn and I figured we were on a gravel road. A fine coating of dust began to drift in through the windows and settle on me. Road grime and the occasional dried mud ball grew thick enough that I could begin to taste it, on and on we drove.

I drifted back to sleep, or maybe I was just in and out of consciousness, I don't know. Ultimately, we turned off onto some other road that was a couple of notches down from what we'd been on. We couldn't have been traveling more than about ten miles an hour, occasionally slowing down even further for some dip or bump along the way. I could hear branches and things bumping off the side of the vehicle. After maybe twenty minutes of that, we suddenly came to a stop.

"God, it's about fucking time, where in the hell are we anyway?" one of the pair of feet resting on me said then used my head to push off as he climbed out the open door.

The air drifting in on me had a cool, damp feel to it, and I could hear birds that sounded as if they were a good distance off. Their calls seemed to echo. Someone was walking around outside the vehicle and I heard twigs snapping.

"Drag that sack of shit out here," a voice I recognized as Bulldog's said.

Heavy hands suddenly grabbed me by the shoulders, and unceremoniously yanked me out of the vehicle. I felt suspended in mid air for a good second or two, before I bounced off the wet ground with a loud groan. "Uff."

"Just stay down there wise guy," it was Bulldog again, punctuating his statement with a sharp kick to my ribs.

There was a loud creak, and I opened my eyes just enough to see a tailgate drop down on the back of a pickup. Bulldog gave a nod as a large figure crossed into my field of vision and pulled something out of the back of the pickup.

The *something* turned out to be *someone* tied and bound with a hood over his head. As the large body hit the ground it bounced twice and didn't move. This type of activity didn't bode well for my immediate future.

"Think he's dead?" A voice asked then hauled something out of the back of the truck. A moment later I saw two rifle barrels hanging along either side of his legs. I could hear more items being dragged out of the truck, but I remained still, kept my eyes closed and hoped it would all just go away.

"Haul that up to the main cabin, then bring one of them all terrains back down here, and we'll drag these two into the shed. Let em rest up for their big day, tomorrow."

I heard what sounded like a heavy duty lawnmower start a few minutes later then grow louder as it came closer. Somehow I had the idea that if I just lay still they'd leave me alone and maybe go away. It didn't work.

Some jerk rolled me over, wrapped a chain around my legs then hoisted my feet off the ground as he hooked the chain to some sort of bumper hitch. He did the same thing with another chain. Through squinted eyes, I saw the body with the hood pulled over its head roll next to me.

"Let me drive that thing," Bulldog said, and climbed into the seat of the ATV. I opened my eyes just as he turned around with that stupid crooked grin plastered across his face. He raised his eyebrows when he looked down at me and said, "Giddy-up." Then he floored the ATV and took off like a bat out of hell. The chain around my ankles felt like it would pull my legs right out of the hip socket. I rolled from side to side down a sandy trail, bouncing over the occasional tree root, or off the hooded body chained up alongside me.

My hip glanced off a granite boulder, and I bounced over a half dozen more tree roots before we came to a stop. Dust drifted over me and into my eyes, nose, and mouth. I couldn't stop coughing, and rolled to my side, which garnered the sudden attention of someone's boot that placed another swift kick into my ribs.

"No one said you could move, you worthless piece of shit."

Not a problem, I was already doubled over on the ground gasping for breath. It was going to be a while before I'd be ready to go anywhere.

"Lock these two fucks in the shed, chain 'em up to one of them beam's. Then come on up to the cabin," Bulldog said. With that, the ATV accelerated down the trail. I half expected to be dragged behind again, and waited for the chain to yank my legs out of the hip socket. Instead, a pair of hands grabbed me by my ankles, and dragged me thru an overhead door, into some sort of shelter. I felt myself get yanked up onto a concrete pad, and then get dragged another twenty feet.

My legs were suddenly pulled up into the air, and over my continual groaning, I heard the sound of a chain being wrapped around something over head. There were at least two guys, and they did the same thing to the other body, then seemed to chuckle. One of them said, "Let's grab a beer," as if they'd just finished some yard work. Then the overhead door closed and I was lying in the dark on a concrete floor with my legs chained up in the air. Occasionally I heard a muffled sort of groan from somewhere off to the side, but it was too dark to see anything.

I grew thirsty, and my head was pounding after being in the same position for God knows how long. A couple of times I croaked out a question, "Are you alive over there?" But I never got a response. Sometime later, the door was pulled open and a guy staggered in. I was either asleep, or flat out unconscious, until he kicked me with the toe of his boot.

"Something to get your strength up for the games tomorrow," he laughed, then poured what I think was a beer over me. I was parched, and attempted to lick up as much of the cold liquid as I could. My legs had gone completely numb. I couldn't tell if I was wiggling my toes or not. About the only thing I could feel was a savage pounding in my head.

Chapter Thirty-Five

I thought it might be daybreak. I could see a hint of gray light creaking through the slit at the bottom of the door. Something small scurried in front it, a mouse, or maybe a rat. I was more numb than not, and very cold. Over the course of time, the light outside brightened, and I could begin to make out some blurry images.

It looked like we were in some sort of large storage shed. There were a number of fifty-five gallon drums, various tools, shovels, odd pieces of lumber, and what looked like a cement mixer. A stack of tires were piled one on top of the other, over in a far corner. I could make out the grill and headlights of some dark-colored vehicle, way in the back of the place. Whoever was lying next to me was awfully still, although I could detect some breathing. I could just barely make out the hood pulled over his head.

There must have been a sheet metal roof on the place, because there was the occasional hollow echo as a twig bounced off, or a bird landed and walked around before flying away. There were a few small nail holes where daylight attempted to shine through, but nothing that could be considered effective illumination.

I heard their voices from some distance off. The hum of conversation, but still too far away to discern what was actually being said. A minute or two later, the sound of their footsteps came into range, the occasional snapped twig, kicked dirt, and then the pounding of feet on the concrete pad, just before the door was pulled open.

For a brief moment, bright light flooded in the open door then three large figures strode in blocking out most of the light, and throwing me back into the shadows.

"Get 'em down or they won't be worth shit on the course this afternoon." It was Bulldog's voice, and I immediately tried to feign unconsciousness. I felt my legs being raised even higher for a moment, and just as I was about to let out a groan, they dropped like a rock, and bounced off the concrete floor. Pain shot up my spine, and exploded at the base of my skull like fireworks going off. When the legs on the body next to me hit the concrete floor, he let out an audible groan.

"Make sure he's still breathing, or we'll just be left with worthless Haskell, here," Bulldog said.

Someone set a five gallon plastic pail on the floor. The pail was white, with red and blue lettering on it, although I couldn't make out what it said.

"Some food to get your strength back," Bulldog laughed, then said, "Come on, we gotta get the course ready, they're gonna be up here in about an hour." They all left and locked the door behind them. The sound of their conversation, and the occasional laughter quickly drifted away, until it was just the two of us alone again in the dark.

The fat figure lying on the floor coughed, but didn't seem to move. I forced myself to sit up, and had a good deal of trouble getting into the position. I dragged myself over to one of the metal barrels, and leaned my back against it. I began to massage my legs in an attempt to get the blood flowing again. I could feel my heart beat pounding through my eyeballs.

Eventually sensation in my legs and feet started to return. I think I was able to wiggle my toes, but I couldn't be sure. I began to feel a number of sharp pains, instead of one giant dull pain. Maybe that was progress.

Across the way in the dark, the body let out a groan, but I was too focused on my immediate survival to strike up a conversation. After a bit, I smelled something tantalizing, and thought at first I must be hallucinating, but the smell remained. I pulled the white plastic pail toward me, and the sensation increased. It was somewhat sweet, and on a better day in different circumstances, I probably could have identified it. I reached my hand in, and felt something warm in the bottom of the pail. It was food.

I guessed they'd used the pail as a scrap bucket, which made this a little like feeding hogs. They must have scraped their pans and plates into the bucket, then carried the thing down here, not that I was in a position to take offense. The identifiable smell of food made me instantly ravenous and I reached down, grabbed a handful, sniffed once more, before I quickly stuffed it into my mouth.

Pancakes I think, with syrup. Maybe some eggs, the occasional bit of sausage. I took a second larger handful and stuffed it into my mouth, then spit out the remnants of a paper napkin, or maybe a paper towel, and threw it off to the side.

I leaned back against the steel drum, and closed my eyes. My head throbbed, and I could hear my stomach beginning to churn on the first bit of food I'd had in a good twenty-four hours.

There was a groan off to my left a while later, followed by some coughing. It was still too dark to really see any detail. I could barely make out a figure rolling back and forth a few times. I called out "Are you okay?" But I never got a reply. Under the circumstances, it probably wasn't the brightest of questions to ask.

There were voices outside again, and car doors slamming. I must have fallen asleep because I jerked awake. I couldn't make out what was being said, other than what sounded like a lot of back slapping and laughing. A dog barked, maybe two dogs. They sounded big.

The noise gradually faded away, and I was left listening to the figure just a few feet away, groan and cough in the dark. Eventually he took a couple of deep breaths, coughed a few times then said, "Shit."

I couldn't disagree. "How you doing?" I asked.

"Christ almighty, how long, where the hell is this?"

"Can't help you, pal."

"My head's killing me, I can barely move my leg, some bastard kicked me a while back. God, I hurt all over."

"I didn't know if you were alive or dead with that hood over your face."

"That damn piss ant Bulldog, he likes to do that, cover your eyes then take cheap shots at you knowing you can't hit back. Always plays the tough guy when he has plenty of back up. I get my hands on that son-of-a-bitch he's dead."

"They keep talking about a run this afternoon. Any idea what that's about?"

"A run?"

"Yeah."

"Don't mean nothing to me. Can you see anything? Is there a way out of this place?"

"They had us chained up over night. I'm just now beginning to get some feeling back in my legs. I haven't tried to stand yet. A way out? God, I doubt it," I said.

"I'm starving, I'd give my right arm for a couple of Big Mac's and some beer."

I didn't say anything. The scrap bucket they'd brought down was empty. I hadn't planned on him coming back to life.

Chapter Thirty-Six

We didn't say anything for probably an hour. Both of us just sat there in a lot of pain, and without any idea what in the hell to do. You hear about someone in this type of situation and you think, *'I know what I'd do. I wouldn't let them do that to me. I'd escape. I'd fight back. I'd have a Samurai sword and lop off their heads in one fell swoop'*. But when you're faced with the actual circumstance it isn't that simple, or maybe it is. I suppose we could have grabbed something, a shovel, maybe find a hammer or pick up a board. Then again, apparently he couldn't walk because they'd hurt his leg, which left me. I suppose I could charge them, try and get to that sadist Bulldog, if one of them didn't shoot me first. They mentioned a run. I thought maybe I could hide in the woods or climb a tree, and just hope they wouldn't find me.

I heard them from a good distance off, the dogs, barking and running. From the sound of their barking, they seemed to run past and then around the building. They scratched their paws against the steel garage door, and barked some more. The noise echoed through the dark where we'd been dumped. I could see the shadow from their feet in the sliver of light, between the concrete pad and the bottom of the door. The noise of conversation and casual yelling grew louder. Someone laughed, and an engine started from a ways off, then grew louder as it approached. It didn't think it was a car or a motorcycle, it sounded smaller, like a scooter or something. Whatever it was drove past the door, and faded off to the right. A second one followed shortly after. A moment later the overhead door went up, this time there were a half dozen silhouettes stepping toward us, way too many for my Samurai sword fantasy.

"Put a pillowcase over shit-for-brains Haskell's head, just in case." I recognized Bulldog's voice, as someone grabbed me by the hair, and yanked my head forward. I guess it was a pillowcase that was slipped over my head then tightened around my neck with a rope or something.

I heard the other guy groan, "Oh Jesus, no, please don't do this, please."

"Shut the hell up," Bulldog sneered, then there was a sort of thunk sound and the guy groaned. Bulldog probably hit or kicked him. I figured with the hood over our heads, this was the part where Bulldog felt comfortable beating us up.

"Listen up, you two pieces of shit. Think about doing anything, and we'll shoot your ass just as sure as I'm standing here. Believe me, nothing would please me more. Now, Tubby likes to play his games, so that's exactly what you're going to do here. Okay, get their ass in gear," he snarled.

With that two pairs of hands grabbed me by the arms, and hoisted me to my feet. I had difficulty walking, so they half dragged, half walked me out of the building. I couldn't see, but I could sense the sunlight through the pillowcase, and felt some warmth from the sun.

A few stumbles later and my shins hit something hard. I started to tumble forward, when someone gave me a swift push from behind, and I landed hard on some sort of flat surface. I felt a metal frame, and a then wood base, but just as I was feeling around, the other guy was dropped on top of me, which brought a chorus of loud laughter from the assembled idiots.

"Get your damn legs up there, or they'll get run over." A voice yelled then the other guy with the hood got half rolled on top of me, and groaned in pain.

"Looks like they got to know one another better than we thought last night," some other fool chuckled, which brought on more laughter from everyone.

"Okay, get their worthless asses up there."

I recognized Bulldog's now familiar growl. He'd barely finished speaking, when a motor fired up and we were moving. We must have been on some sort of flat bed trailer thing. I tried to remain still, and not fall off although it was next to impossible. It felt like we were traveling about eighty-miles-an-hour, and hitting every bump along the trail. I had the sense we were traveling uphill.

We drove for quite a few minutes. I was tempted to try and rip off the pillowcase, but it was wrapped so tight around my neck, I was afraid I'd choke. Well, that and the fact I didn't feel any great need to be staring into the barrel of some idiot's gun.

We suddenly made a sharp, sort of U-turn and came to an abrupt stop. The sudden stop slid me forward across the wooden base, and I felt slivers tear into the palms of my hands and my knees. We were parked at some sort of angle, and I half rolled to the edge.

"Get the hell off of there," a voice said. Hands suddenly grabbed me by the belt and my collar, and tossed me onto the ground. I rolled a few times, and figured we were on a hill. I heard a thud and a groan. A second later the other guy rolled into me.

"Best take them hoods off and let 'em enjoy the view," someone said.

I heard some rustling next to me and then a hushed expletive. "Fucking hell."

A moment later the pillowcase was ripped off my head, and I had to blink a half dozen times to get my eyes adjusted. There was a red, all-terrain four-wheeler with a small flat bed trailer about ten feet further up the hill. Two guys were just walking away from it. One of them had tribal sort of tattoos circling his very large biceps.

We were in the middle of a hillside with trees maybe twenty-five yards away on either side and behind us. Down at the base of the hill, there were maybe a half dozen figures. I could make out Bulldog, I think Ben was there, Tubby was seated in a chair holding court next to a large table with an umbrella in the middle of it. His hair glistened in the sun, like a shinny copper helmet and he drank from a stemmed glass. The table had a number of plates with what looked like different types of hors d'oeuvres, and ice buckets with a variety of bottles jammed into them. There were three rifles set up on tripods in front of the group and what looked like beach blankets spread out on the ground behind the weapons.

The group started to suddenly whoop and laugh, and point off to the right. I turned and watched the two guys I'd seen a moment before roll out a giant plastic ball from behind a small shack. It stood maybe eight-feet-tall, clear plastic, and bounced like it was inflated.

As they came closer, I realized it was a double walled sort of thing and large enough so someone could crawl inside.

"That there's a Tumble Bubble," a voice chuckled from behind. "We're about to have us some fun," he laughed.

I looked at him with a mixture of abject fear and incredulity. He wore a Cubs' baseball cap, jeans, and T-shirt with a Batman logo. Neither the jeans, nor the T-shirt, looked to have been washed in the past month or two.

"It's your one chance, hot shot. All you got to do is make it to them trees 'fore they shoot your worthless ass, and you're home free. Your buddy here'll show you how it's done," he said. then reached down and tore the pillowcase off the head of the other guy.

I blinked and couldn't believe my eyes. He was still in the dirty jeans and T-shirt I'd last seen him in when he'd tried to shoot me. I'd reached into his passenger side window and grabbed the snub .38 out of his hands. He face was swollen and pretty black and blue. "Jace?"

"You, Haskell? If it weren't for you I wouldn't be here. You're the one who got me in all this trouble. You're the one done this to me," he said, then pointed at his right leg. Even through the jeans, it was obvious his knee was clearly swollen and looked to be about the size of his thigh.

"Sorry, but looks like you two ain't going to get any time to strike up an old friendship," Batman chuckled. With that, the two guys rolled up with the large plastic ball, and Batman pulled a nasty looking automatic from behind his back and pointed it at Jace. "Best get your ass in there, Jace."

"Reggie, come on, man, I can barely walk. You gotta tell 'em down there. Cut me some slack, man, we're pals."

"Can't do it, Jace. You know how they are. Now get your ass in there, or I'll shoot you myself. And I mean it, I will."

"Reggie!" Jace pleaded.

"Get in there, man, come on do it," he said, then pointed the pistol at Jace's head. I had no doubt he'd pull the trigger if he had to.

One of the two guys holding the large ball stepped over and grabbed Jace by the hair. "Come on, fat ass. This'll all be over soon enough. Just get your ass in there, damn it," he said, then dragged Jace by the hair over to a hole where he was supposed to climb into the giant inflated ball.

"Ahhh, God, my knee, damn it, my knee. Hold on, now just hold on a damn minute, here. Were you listening? I just got done telling you I can barely walk."

"Jace," Reggie said. "Get in there, and I'll give you a good push toward the trees, but you gotta do it, man. You ain't got a choice. Now come on."

Jace groaned, then began to wiggle and struggle through the small hole into the interior of the ball. "I can't, Reggie. I can't." Then he screamed, "You did this, Haskell. This is all your fault. None of this would be happening if it wasn't for you. You hear me, Haskell, you hear me?"

The guy with the tattooed biceps kicked him hard in the rear a couple of times as an added incentive. Jace's voice echoed inside the large ball, then became muffled as he attempted to stand up. I could see his lips moving, saw the rage in his face, he was looking around wildly, screaming, but it was impossible to hear him.

"They ain't quite set up down there, Jace. So I'm going to give you a head start with a good push toward them trees. You just keep going, boy and don't stop, you might just make it there, and if you do they let you go. Them's the rules. You just go like hell and don't look at 'em any. Okay?"

Jace turned his head and looked at Batman with a frightened, pleading look on his face. I couldn't hear him so it looked like he mouthed a final plea and screamed, "Reggie."

Down at the base of the hill, there was suddenly a lot of shouting and scurrying around by everyone except Tubby, who remained oozing out of his chair, and in the process of refilling his stemmed glass.

Reggie and the other two guys started pushing the large ball with Jace inside, picking up speed. They trotted alongside rolling the giant plastic ball and directing it with their hands. Then they gave it a final push toward the tree line, and Jace bounced around inside. It looked like he was screaming, but you couldn't hear anything. Almost immediately, a shot was fired from the crowd down at the bottom of the hill. The sound echoed off the tree line, and seemed to bounce back and forth across the surrounding hills.

"Jesus Christ," one of the guys yelled, as all three of them hit the ground. I rolled over face down and remained perfectly still.

Jace bounced in the general direction of the tree line, as he attempted to get to his feet and run inside the giant ball. He was moving his hands, and then sort of collapsed inside the ball. He moved into a crawling position, all the while trying to maintain some momentum, as he attempted to roll across the hill toward the distant trees, and his supposed safety. He looked to be failing miserably.

Two puffs of dirt clipped the ground, maybe five feet in front of the ball. That seemed to get Jace's attention, and he began sort of crawling and paddling for all he was worth. More rounds were fired, but I was unable to tell where they were hitting. There was a lot of whopping and laughter going on behind the shooters.

Suddenly there was a large red splatter on the inside of the ball, and a cheer rose up from the crowd at the bottom of the hill. Jace sort of flipped over on his back, holding his arm at the wrist. The hand at the end of the wrist was mostly gone. His mouth stretched wide open in an inaudible scream. He made an attempt to get up, and two more splatters quickly showered the inside of the ball.

He began to roll downhill for a bit, but stopped after a few feet as the ball quickly deflated and came to a stop. Then it just sat there, and gradually oozed down over his body as maybe a dozen more rounds were fired. Some kicked up dirt in front of Jace and the deflated ball, the rest may have hit their target or sailed off into the atmosphere. It was impossible to tell.

"Well, hot shot, I'd guess you sort of get the idea. That ain't exactly how you'd want to do it, though," Reggie laughed. "Go get that other one, fellas," he said, then leveled his automatic at me. "You just stay put on the ground 'til they get back, Haskell."

Chapter Thirty-Seven

I took a panicked look around the hillside, and then suddenly felt a weird sort of calm drift over me. So this was where I was going to die. I'd seen worse places, a lot of them, more than my share as a matter of fact, but damn it. I looked down at the assembled crowd at the base of the hill, I could hear the sound of congratulations and saw them giving high fives to one another, but couldn't make out the specifics of what was being said.

I recognized one of the shooters as she filled her champagne glass. I'd taken her out before, even bought her champagne. Pink champagne, if I recalled correctly. Crickett.

I heard a noise and turned. The guy with the tribal tattoos and his pal where rolling another giant ball over my way. They stopped and adjusted it so I'd be able to crawl up and into the thing through the little hole. All sorts of comparisons began to flood my mind.

"Your turn, Haskell, but I got to tell you the truth. Even if you do make it to them trees way over there, we ain't gonna let you go. What would be the point?" Batman laughed. "You dumb shit, you sure as hell messed with the wrong people."

I just sat there with a few thousand thoughts flashing through my thick skull, *'Things I didn't do, things I shouldn't have done, things I was sorry for.'*

"Get him on his feet, they look about ready down there. We'll give him a push or two, then get the hell out of the way. Someone's fast on the trigger down there."

"I think it's the bitch," the other guy said then pulled me up by the collar wheeled me around and pushed me forward.

I fell to my knees in front of the ball, and one of them kicked me hard in the rear a couple of times, directing me with his boot in through the little entry hole. A number of parallel images flashed through my mind.

"Enjoy the run, dumb shit," Batman chuckled.

I looked frantically at the two of them, but they were all smiles, actually enjoying the situation.

I glanced down the hill, and saw the small crowd of people milling around. Someone was already lying down in a prone position behind one of the weapons, although at an odd angle. Not that I had time to worry. Batman shouted something, but I couldn't make it out. They gave me a little push, just barely enough to get me going. I felt like I was the proverbial sitting duck. I frantically attempted to get my feet and hands moving in some coordinated effort. It felt like I was sitting there for an hour, but I began to pick up speed and move in the general direction of the tree line. It looked more like twenty-five miles away instead of the twenty-five yards I'd estimated earlier.

My hands and feet squeaked against the plastic walls. A couple of times I lost my balance, but rolled back up into position. I was essentially inside a giant ball, running and paddling for all I was worth. I couldn't hear any of their shots, but I had no doubt they were firing. *'Stay focused, just get to the trees, just keep moving, faster, faster'* I screamed inside my head.

I gave another quick glance down the hill, and the one guy was still in that awkward prone position. Another clown was lying on his back with his feet toward the rifle, like he planned to shoot at me with his toes or something. *'Just keep clowning pal, I'm halfway there.'*

I glanced again and noticed everyone was running, running very fast as a matter of fact, away from the chairs, the table with the umbrella, the snacks, and the ice buckets with champagne. Even Tubby was up and waddling as fast as he could go.

Bulldog drove up alongside him, and Tubby draped himself across the rear seat and shouted something. Crickett tried to grab on, but Tubby kicked her away, and Bulldog quickly sped off.

Someone next to Crickett dropped to the ground, and for a moment she just stood there staring at him, looking shocked before she took off running. I kept on paddling for all I was worth until I made it into the tree line. I rolled the giant ball in between a couple of birch trees, then angled my way back out the small hole. Halfway up the hill, Batman was lying face down, and very still. His two pals were running for all they were worth into the distant tree line.

It looked like chaos down at the bottom of the hill. A couple of the ice buckets were knocked over, Tubby's chair was tipped on its side, stemmed glasses were scattered, and paper napkins were blowing all over. One of the all-terrain vehicles was overturned with a pair of legs sticking out from underneath. The odd angled guy and the fellow with his feet pointed toward the rifle remained on the ground, where they'd fallen. A dark pool had formed around the head of the fellow at the odd angle. About fifteen feet from those two, was someone else face down. Further down the trail, there was a body on the ground that looked to still be twitching, but wasn't getting anywhere.

Chapter Thirty-Eight

Including Batman on the hillside, I counted six individuals down. Apparently shot. Plus Jace, who was still close to the top of the hill in the deflated bubble. My immediate thought was to get the hell away from here as fast and as far as possible. I cautiously crept down the hill through the woods then traveled parallel with the trail, staying about ten yards into the woods.

I knelt down behind a large tree, and studied the body lying in the middle of the trail, by now it had stopped twitching. The only sounds I could hear was the occasional screech of some far off bird, and the growing sound of flies buzzing. More and more flies.

I continued to study the body and the area around me for some time. I couldn't see anyone moving, didn't see any birds suddenly flutter up, and couldn't detect a flash off a metal object on someone hiding in the woods.

I cautiously approached the body on the trail. The entrance wound in the back of his head was smaller than a dime. I half rolled him over. The exit wound was close to the size of my fist, and had taken out the entire left side of his forehead. He must have been dead before he hit the ground. I pulled a pistol from his waistband that looked like a Walther, but sitting there in the middle of the trail I didn't feel like taking time to study the piece. I crouched as I ran, and hurried back into the brush.

I followed the trail again, moving parallel with it, and still about ten yards into the forest. The trail gradually wound its way down toward a valley floor, to a cleared area with a long gravel drive and a number of out buildings. Further on, I could just make out a massive boulder and log structure that I took to be a cabin of some sort, large and elegant.

Two small shacks, barely the size of a brothel bedroom, but with front porches sat off to the right. There was a rocker on one porch and a couple of broken aluminum lawn chairs on the other. Both structures appeared to be uninhabited and looked unused for quite some time. Opposite the shacks, was a building with a metal garage door, and a concrete pad in front of the door. The roof of the place was simple, corrugated sheet metal, most likely the structure where Jace and I had been held over night.

I crouched in the underbrush, waiting for what seemed like hours searching for any movement. There were a series of car tire tracks where the soil had been chewed up, indicating vehicles had spun out at a high speed. After a long wait, I gradually made my way through the forest, toward the large cabin. It looked more and more like a fortress as I approached.

The structure was three stories high, and built with the back and one side burrowed into a slight rise. The other side and the front were lined with massive field stones rising up maybe ten feet. Above the field stone huge, peeled logs rose up another two stories. The gutters and downspouts were copper, the roof looked to be slate, and featured six dormers, each with a pair of lace curtained windows. A large screened porch sat on the far end of the structure, and a stone patio spread out beyond that. An imposing staircase of red, granite slabs led up to a porch running the length of the second floor. Centered in the log wall, was a pair of French doors with leaded, beveled glass windows. The side near me, featured a metal garage door, and next to that a side door. As far as I could determine the place was empty. I grasped the pistol I'd pulled off the body back on the trail and waited behind a large pine tree all the same.

It gradually grew dark, but no lights came on inside the cabin. It was damp, cool heading toward chilly, and very quiet. I heard some noise off to the left, and watched as three deer strolled into view. They nibbled at some leaves, then hopped a few steps, seemed to sniff the air, then nibbled some more, and repeated the process. Over the course of fifteen or twenty minutes they made their way past the cabin and gradually faded deeper into the forest.

After another hour, I still had seen nothing suggesting any movement from inside, and I was getting cold. The last thing I'd eaten had been the breakfast scraps in the five gallon pail hours ago. Not for the first time my stomach rumbled, and if anyone was out there hunting me, I figured they were bound to hear it.

An hour later, and it was full on night. I was unable to stop shivering, I'd grown so cold. Still, the cabin was dark. Sometimes, people get so desperate, they don't care what the consequences might be. That's the point I was at. I simply didn't care. Over the course of the day things had distilled down to the basics and right now I needed food and some shelter.

I cautiously approached the walk-in side door, and listened with my ear up against it straining for sound, any sound. The only thing I heard was my stomach rumbling and my teeth chattering. I cautiously turned the door handle, and it opened. I stepped back to the side, away from the door, carefully pushed it open with my foot, and waited. Nothing.

I couldn't tell if my shivering was from the cold, or due to stark fear. I almost didn't care. I just wanted to get inside and find something to eat. I stepped inside, crouched down, and listened. A moment or two later, I pulled the door closed behind me. Although it was dark, moonlight filtering through the window suggested I was in some sort of workshop. I could make out a table saw, and various tools on what looked like a work bench. Lengths of lumber were stacked along the floor, and there was the slight hint of a pine smell in the air.

I felt my way across the room and came to another door. I turned the handle and again it was unlocked. I quietly opened the door and stepped through. In the moonlight I could just make out a staircase off to my left, rising up to the main floor. Except for the sound of my stomach rumbling I waited quietly in a dark corner. I continued to listen for something, anything.

The staircase rose up eight steps to a landing, then reversed direction for another eight steps. The steps were built from peeled logs and solid as a rock, not giving out so much as a creak as I warily crept up to the landing. I crouched on the landing for a good five minutes, but didn't hear anything. I softly crept up the next eight steps, waiting at the top for the slightest sound. My stomach continued to rumble loudly.

"That you, Dev?"

I froze.

I heard a round being chambered and a very serious voice called out, "Tell me it's Dev Haskell, or you're dead."

"It's me, it's me, Jesus, don't shoot."

"God damn it, Dev, it took you long enough, it's me, Charlie. Up here."

I looked up toward the open two-story ceiling as Charlie Bergstrom swung down from a log beam. He hung there by his arms swaying slightly from side to side, then dropped to the ground and landed in a sort of crouch.

"Good God," he groaned standing up and stretching from side to side. "I wasn't sure you were ever going to make it in here. I'm getting way too old for this shit."

He was dressed in a camouflage of some sort, his face, neck, and hands were painted, and nearly impossible to distinguish in the dark, the whites of his eyes shown in the moonlight. He had a long rifle with a very large scope mounted on it slung over his shoulder.

"What the hell took you?" he asked.

"I wanted to make sure it was safe. Jesus Christ, was that you out there? The shooting?"

"You mean breaking up the little party they had planned for you? What a bunch of animals. You see what they did to that poor bastard bouncing around in that thing. Damn, and he was one of their own. I saw that, figured you had about a zero chance of making it. I was so busy knocking them down, old lard ass got away. Say, you hungry? Man, I could eat a small child. Let's see what they got here. Oh, maybe don't turn on any lights, and under the circumstances probably best not to leave any fingerprints. Here," he said, and reached into a side pocket halfway down his thigh. "Better slip these on." He handed me what looked like surgical gloves.

"How did you get here? How'd you know that I…Charlie what in the hell is going on?"

Chapter Thirty-Nine

He stared at me for a moment like he was gauging his response, maybe determining exactly how much I could handle. "Been a pretty busy day, let's see what they got to eat. Then we better get the hell out of here. Come on, kitchen's this way," he said, then turned and walked down a hallway.

I followed a few steps behind. He walked past a couple of dark rooms, then made a left and stepped into a kitchen. The moonlight illuminated the room, shining off the granite counter tops and the light colored walls. "You got those gloves on?"

"Yeah."

"Check those drawers, see if you can find some plastic bags or something to carry some food in. Probably best if we make tracks pretty damn fast, they're bound to return with reinforcements."

I started pulling open drawers, the fourth or fifth drawer held aluminum foil, Saran Wrap and a box of Ziploc bags. I handed the box to Charlie.

"Wow, high class. Never would of guessed it," he said, and opened the refrigerator door. The light immediately went on, and he quickly reached into the far back corner and unscrewed the bulb. "There, let's see, looks like we got some ribs or something here. I think this is chicken." He placed two large platters on the counter. What's this? No," he said and pushed some large jar off to the side. "You want Coke or it looks like some sort of sport drink thing."

"Coke is fine."

"Okay," he said hauling out a couple of cans and setting them on the counter. "Let's get the hell out of here. What'd you touch coming in?"

"Touch?"

"Yeah, you leave any fingerprints?"

"Ahhh, I think just the door knobs."

"That all? You're sure?"

"Yeah, just the knobs, that door at the bottom of the stairs, and the one coming into that workshop or whatever it is."

"Then let's go," he said. He emptied the platters into the bags, handed them to me, and we headed down the stairs. He had a rag of some sort in his hand, and he polished the door knob on both sides of the door by the staircase. "Wait for me outside," he instructed as we made our way through the workshop.

I cautiously opened the door and waited a moment. I didn't see or hear anything, but then again it was dark, and there were a few million places to hide. I stepped outside then crouched down against the fieldstone foundation, feeling like I was sitting under a bright spotlight. Charlie stepped out of the door a moment later, wiped the knob, and quietly pulled the door closed. I was up, and took a couple of steps down the lane toward the shacks.

He grabbed my arm and signaled another direction, then stepped off and I followed a few paces behind. We made our way through the dark forest for the better part of an hour without saying a word. We came to a small rise, and I heard the sound of water rushing over rocks from somewhere off to the left, not too far away.

Charlie stopped and waved me forward, then leaned in close to my ear, and whispered. "I've got a vehicle up here just a couple of clicks. I want you to get in it and drive to my place."

"I don't have the slightest idea where in the hell we are," I whispered.

"I've got a GPS in my truck, just set it for Vaxholm, Minnesota and it'll get you there."

My blank look spoke volumes.

"Jesus Christ, you don't know how to program a GPS?"

"I can barely send a text message on my phone." I said.

"God, all right, I'll set it up for you."

"What about you?"

"Once I get you out of here, I won't be far behind. I've got another vehicle. You just get to my place, wait for me there. Give me one of those bags of food, whichever one you don't want."

"Doesn't matter to me, I'm so hungry I really don't care what I eat."

He yanked a bag from beneath my arm, and waved me forward. We halted, and Charlie told me to wait until he came back for me, then he slithered off to the right, and disappeared into the dark forest a moment later. He came back for me about ten minutes after that.

"Come on, it looks clear, let's get you the hell out of here," he whispered, and led the way.

His truck was parked in a cleared area, just a few yards off the road. The GPS was mounted on his dash and he was pushing buttons. "You know, I'd tell you what I'm doing, explain it to you, but I've got the feeling that right now, it would just go in one ear and out the other. No offense."

"No offense taken," I said.

He stepped back and made an elegant wave of his hand, "Get your ass in there, and just listen to the lady. I should be about twenty minutes behind you. Can you find my place once you get to Vaxholm?"

"Yeah, I'll be there waiting for you. Hey, Charlie, thanks, man. I mean you saved my life."

He nodded slightly, gave me a long look then said, "Haskell, you're the only son-of-a-bitch that cared for Daryl, tried to help. I appreciate that, and I know in his own way he would have, too. Better get moving, it's almost a three-hour drive," he said, then stepped back, closed the door on the truck, and faded into the woods.

I pulled out onto the road, and listened to the directions from the nice sounding lady. It was a little after midnight according to the digital on the dash. I opened the plastic bag of food on the passenger seat and reached in. Ribs, and lots of them.

Chapter Forty

By the time I reached Charlie's place I was fighting to stay awake, and considering passing thoughts like *'I'll just close my eyes for a minute or two.'* Not the best idea when you're ripping along an unfamiliar state highway at close to seventy miles per hour. The sexy voice coming across the GPS sort of brought me back to semi-consciousness. "Turn right in six hundred feet."

I was coming into the east side of Vaxholm, a quiet little town just about any time of the day. At close to four in the morning, the only semblance of life was a flickering street light just outside of the Citizens Bank. I slowed to the speed limit, and drove through the main street of town in just over a minute. It was wide enough to accommodate the herds of cattle or flocks of sheep from a hundred and forty years ago when the majority of the two-story brick buildings had been built. I passed the white frame Lutheran church where Daryl's funeral was held and continued out onto a county road. After a little more than a mile, I turned onto the road that led to Charlie's place.

There weren't any street lights out here. I passed a couple of farms with a light on over the barn. The fields were planted with a crop I couldn't identify in the dark or, since I was a city kid and couldn't tell, maybe had already been harvested. I pulled onto the private gravel road that led into Charlie's and followed the drive up to his place. I parked at an angle so he couldn't possibly miss me. Then I scrounged around behind the seat and found a fleece blanket. I laid the Walther next to me on the passenger seat, and closed my eyes for just a minute.

The pounding on the driver's window jerked me awake, and I blinked Charlie into focus. It was daylight. Not early morning daylight, but rather more respectable, like a banker's ten o'clock kind of daylight.

"This is getting to be a bad habit of yours. Well, come on you better get out, 'spose I'll have to make you breakfast again," he said, and headed for the kitchen door.

I groaned from behind the steering wheel and stretched in an attempt to get some of the kinks out, then followed him into the house. It dawned on me that he had cleaned up and was dressed in jeans, a flannel shirt, and looked to be freshly shaved.

"What time is it?" I asked.

"Past ten, good Lord, the morning's half over, and you haven't accomplished a damn thing yet."

"I made it here without taking a side trip into the ditch."

"Yeah, I guess you did. Look no offense, but a shower wouldn't do you any harm." Then his voice softened, and he said, "You can help yourself to any of Daryl's clothes."

I nodded thanks, then headed for the bathroom. A long, hot, steaming shower can do wonders for rejuvenation, even if it lasts for only an hour or so. We finished breakfast, and talked about everything except the subject at hand. The kitchen was sunny, and I looked out onto the deck where I'd had my previous breakfast with him. Finally I said, "Charlie, you still haven't told me how you came to be there."

He stood up and started clearing breakfast dishes, then labored at the kitchen sink with his back to me. When he'd finished with the dishes, he stared out the kitchen window at the deck, and the forest beyond. Finally he said, "You know the more I tried to figure this out, the more things seemed to always come back to the same couple of folks. Your pal Gustafson, his…"

"I think you can safely assume we aren't friends."

"His kid, Ben. That worthless slut, Crickett and that deranged idiot with the crew cut and the face that would keep a plastic surgeon awake at night."

"I think you mean Bulldog."

"Mmm-mmm, that bastard got a real name?"

"If he does I've never heard it."

He turned round and looked at me, leaned against the granite counter and folded his arms across his chest. "I sort of poked around a little, looking for I don't know what. I don't think I'll ever be able to link them to Daryl's murder, at least not in a way that would stand up in court. But that doesn't mean they weren't involved."

I nodded, and said, "I had a pleasant chat with Tubby's kid, Ben. He said the two of them, he and Daryl, were aware that van was being watched by the police. He suggested Daryl took the van more or less on a dare. Figured he either wouldn't get caught, or he could talk his way out of it."

Charlie looked off somewhere in the distance, maybe twenty-plus years ago. A little boy was laughing and shrieking as Charlie chased him around the backyard, then scooped the little guy up and smothered

189

him with kisses. He shook his head ever so slightly, and softly whispered, "Jesus."

"The way Tubby's kid told it, they figured if they could get the police to turn over the cocaine to the DEA, the weak point would be the actual transfer and, well that's seems to be what happened. They somehow found out when the transfer was going to be, or maybe it was as simple as being parked across the street and waiting until the DEA pulled up," I said putting some distance between me and my stupid phone call to Tubby.

"Anyway, they or someone, hijacked the entire thing. I started nosing around, actually found the stash, and called it in. The cops just didn't get there in time."

"What?"

"Yeah, that guy in the big ball, the one they killed, his name was Jace. He was the one supposedly guarding everything in a garage, and I tricked him into letting me in. That's why they shot the poor bastard, he lost their big score. God only knows where it is now."

Charlie sort of shrugged his shoulders, and then began to load the dishwasher. "Probably already out on the street by now," he said, but he didn't sound too convinced. "Look, why don't you help yourself to the bed in Daryl's old room, catch some sleep. I don't see any hurry in getting you back to the city, at least not until we're sure it's safe."

"What about the carnage back at that cabin? There anything about it on the news?"

Charlie shook his head. "I'll lay you odds you won't hear a thing. I'm willing to bet that mess was cleaned up before daybreak. Once they returned with reinforcements, it would have been priority number one. Based on the game they were playing, those big balls they had you two in, I'd say its most likely not the first time something like that went down. God only knows how many folks might be buried out in those woods. Private land like that and lots of it, those are bodies that most likely will never be found."

"Jesus Christ."

"I'd say he wasn't much involved," Charlie said, then seemed to smile to himself.

Chapter Forty-One

I was dead to the world for more than a few hours. I woke sometime in the late afternoon then strolled through the house looking for Charlie, but he was nowhere to be found, so I wandered outside. His truck was just where I'd parked it. I called his name a couple of times and got no answer. I checked the garage, but it was locked. I walked behind the house past the deck and the groomed back lawn out toward the forest, and called his name again with the same result.

I walked back around the house, on a whim I peeked in a side window of the three-stall garage. There were two open bays, and then in the furthest bay I could just make out what looked like a black pickup truck. It was partially covered with a blue tarp that was tied down with a braided yellow cord. Judging from the dirt tracks on the garage floor, it seemed like a pretty safe guess the pickup had been backed in recently, very recently, like maybe early this morning. I was pretty sure I'd seen the vehicle before. Once in the garage Jace had been guarding and then yesterday morning, right before they put the hood over my head and dragged me out. I was sure the thing had been in the back of that storage shed. There were some other events taking precedence at the time so I didn't recognize it, but it looked to be the same vehicle. And, since it was under the blue tarp there was a pretty good chance it was still loaded with the cocaine.

What was it doing at Charlie's? I tried the side door again, but it was locked, the window didn't open, and the three overhead doors were all locked. I climbed up the steps to the front porch, grabbed a rocking chair, and made myself comfortable.

It was almost sundown before Charlie returned. He pulled in driving a white Lexus, gave me a quick wave, then raised the middle garage door and backed in. "You get caught up on some sack time?" he called, lowering the garage door behind him and walking toward me. He was carrying a grocery bag.

"Man, I was out cold."

"Yeah, I popped my head in to check on you, but you looked dead to the world. I got some steaks and a nice Pinot, figured we'd take it easy tonight."

"Sounds fine to me."

"Sit here and enjoy the view. I'm going to get the grill fired up, then I'll come back out. You think you can handle a glass of wine?"

"I'll try my best."

We took our time with a couple of glasses of wine on the front porch, talking about everything other than recent events. Then we made our way out to the back deck where Charlie had the grill going. We were pretty well finished with dinner when Charlie said, "I've got a meeting out here tomorrow morning. I think it might be best if you weren't here while it's going on. Seems to me the less people who know you're out here the better for everyone, especially you."

"You want me to head back to St. Paul?"

"No, I didn't mean it that way. In fact, I think that's a bad idea. A real bad idea, at least until we're sure you'll be safe. I was just thinking, it might make a lot of sense if maybe you went into town or took a long drive. I'd guess you could probably come back around mid-afternoon, maybe call ahead first, just to make sure we're finished. You can take my pickup and see all the sights in the great metropolis of Vaxholm. We got an ice cream store, a grocery store, post office, even got our own police station."

"I think a simple daylight drive in the country might be more to my liking right now."

Charlie nodded like this made a lot of sense.

"Hey Charlie, if you don't mind me asking, I saw that old pickup parked in the garage. What's up with that?"

"Oh, you ever get a bee in your bonnet to do a project, spend some money on the damn thing and it doesn't go any further than that? I was looking to restore that thing. Got it at an auction the next county over. Hell, that must have been two, three years ago, at least. Thus far, about all I've accomplished has been to back it into the garage and throw a tarp over the damn thing."

"I know how that goes. What is that a Ford Ranger?"

"Yep, manufactured right here in Minnesota, as a matter of fact."

"I knew some guys who worked on the line down at the Ford plant in St. Paul. Course that was before they shut it down, first the line, then the entire plant."

"Lot of jobs," Charlie said, and shook his head.

"So you're going to restore it?"

"Theoretically," Charlie said with a laugh then drained his glass.

"Does it run?"

"Tell you the truth, I don't really know, like I said, it's been sitting there for close to two years."

I was thinking of asking about the fresh tire tracks in the garage.

"Dev, if you'll excuse me, I've got some things to attend to in preparation for tomorrow's meeting. Help yourself to anything. I'll get you up for breakfast around seven. My clients will be here by ten, let's play it safe, and have you heading out an hour before that. Okay?"

"Sounds good. To tell you the truth, Charlie. I'm still dragging my ass a bit, I think I'll just turn in."

"Suit yourself," he said, then grabbed our wine glasses and headed into the kitchen.

I was in bed asleep no more than fifteen minutes after that.

Chapter Forty-Two

It wasn't going to take much more before I became addicted to Charlie's pancakes. I ate five of the things for breakfast, stuffed myself into his pickup, and was on the road a few minutes before nine. I drove Northwest with no particular plan in mind other than returning mid-afternoon. I had lunch at a diner that seemed to specialize in high-calorie home cooking. I had the roast beef with mashed potatoes, a gallon of gravy, and green beans. There wasn't so much as a salad or a weight watcher's special on the menu to save your soul.

At sometime during my aimless driving, I noticed what looked like a garage door opener, clipped onto the driver's sun visor in Charlie's pick-up. That got me thinking; *'Who restores a Ford Ranger pickup?'* It didn't seem to make any sense to me. I could see Charlie having some sort of street rod or even a classic car of some sort, but a Ford Ranger? And then I had a problem with that blue tarp and the yellow cord. Maybe that was a coincidence and I was just naïve, if so it was an awfully strange coincidence, not to mention the fresh tire tracks.

Just to play it safe, I returned to Charlie's at more like four in the afternoon. I pulled in alongside the house, then backed toward the garage, and pushed the garage door opener on the visor. The door opened and I quickly backed the pickup in.

No need to hurry. Charlie's White Lexus was in the stall where I'd last seen it and the infamous Ford Ranger was nowhere to be found. The dirt from the tire tracks I'd seen through the window yesterday was gone, swept up I presumed.

Charlie appeared from somewhere in the house maybe an hour later. I was seated at the kitchen counter watching the news and used the remote to turn the volume down when he entered the room.

"So did you see all the sights in our great city?"

"Actually no, I sort of just headed north and west and looked at a lot of lakes."

"That can be enjoyable, too. Anything of interest?"

"A lot of nice scenery, and let's just say the notion of what a lake cabin was when I was a kid has evolved into something totally different today," I said.

"Yeah, I know what you mean. I'm just old enough to question whether that's really progress," Charlie said. He opened the refrigerator, pulled out two beers, nicely chilled, then grabbed a couple of pint glasses out of a cupboard, filled one and pushed it across the counter in my direction.

"Your meeting go okay?" I asked.

"Pretty much, just a timely get together to make sure everyone is on the same page. The phone and email is nice, but every once in awhile you have to be able to look folks in the eye."

I nodded and took a sip. "What exactly is it that you do?"

"Oh, you might say I'm just an entrepreneur. I look for opportunities."

I looked around at the kitchen, oak wood cabinets, stained glass window, granite counter tops, fancy appliances, in floor heating. "Looks like you've found some, opportunities that is."

"Yeah, I've been lucky. Have some good folks who think like I do, and we've been able to work together."

"Construction, high tech, phone apps?"

"Depends on what comes along. What is it Warren Buffet says, he only needs one good idea every year, something like that."

"I think the only quote of his I remember is something about him buying expensive suits, but they still looked cheap on him."

Charlie nodded, then opened the refrigerator again. "I'm thinking salmon fillets tonight. That sound okay to you?"

"As long as I'm not doing the cooking, you could serve up peanut butter and jelly sandwiches and it would be fine with me."

"Let's stick with the salmon fillets. Say, I'm thinking it's probably calmed down enough for you to head back to your place tomorrow."

"Really? This soon? Don't get me wrong, I'm anxious to get back, but it's just been a couple of days. I'm guessing Tubby is out there looking under every rock and trash can trying desperately to find me."

"I have it on good authority that's no longer the case."

"What? Who told you that?"

"I'm really not at liberty to say, but he assures me it's safe for you to return."

"No offense, Charlie, and if I'm cramping your style I get it and it's not a problem, but this seems awfully fast."

"Well, my experience has been this guy, the one I talked to can be trusted. Of course, I'd expect you to check with your own sources, that's just common sense. But, word is your man Tubby has been decimated. Now, I'm going down there to pick up Daryl's son, Oliver, tomorrow. If things check out with your contacts, I can give you a ride back down, and drop you off anywhere you'd like."

"Oliver? How did you ever get Crickett to agree to let you have him? Are you taking him for the weekend, or do you have to submit to one of those supervised visit things?"

"Actually, I'm bringing him back up here, he'll be living with me from now on."

"What about Crickett?"

"She's not my problem, and to be honest, the less I see of her the better. I'm not sure where she'll end up, and as I said, really not my problem. I've decided to place that home on the market. I'll be finalizing some things with the realtor tomorrow, before I pick up the little guy."

"Wow, you must have some really heavy-duty ammunition to get custody of that child."

Charlie just smiled, then unwrapped the package in front of him. Two gorgeous pink fillets glistened on the white butcher paper. "I do these with a chipotle mustard, some brown sugar, and a little lemon. It sounds simple, but I think you'll find it to your liking. You game?"

I nodded, and drained my glass.

"Let me get you a refill there, Dev."

We stepped outside, and Charlie placed the foil-wrapped fillets on the grill. I sat there sipping, and appraising Charlie with a different sense then I had just this morning. I wondered about his inside connection. Was there really one? And what happened to the Ford Ranger pickup? Now, I was even more convinced it was the same one I'd seen in the garage Jace had been guarding. And, Charlie was picking up little Oliver to come live with him, pretty heavy ammunition, very heavy.

Chapter Forty-Three

I phoned Louie the following morning, and told him I'd be in before noon. I didn't have any keys, and wanted to be sure he'd be there. The ride back down to St. Paul wasn't just uneventful, it was boring. Charlie seemed to be deep in thought and answered the couple of questions I asked with just one or two words. I got the message after that, and just stared out the window.

Halfway down, I noticed a red Escalade in the side view mirror. We were on the interstate, and it wouldn't be unusual to have a number of vehicles headed in the same general direction, but this one seemed to keep pace. If we passed someone it pulled out, then tucked back into the right hand lane behind us. The windows were tinted, but I could make out two guys sitting in the front. The third time they followed us passing someone I decided to mention it. "You know that Escalade behind us seems to be right on our ass. Every time you pass someone, they do the same thing, then tuck in right behind us again."

Charlie casually glanced in the rearview mirror, gave a slight smile and said, "I wouldn't let it bother you any, Dev. We got about an hour to go, why don't you tilt that seat back and catch a little nap." The way he said it seemed to be a little stronger than just a simple suggestion, plus I was drowsy, so I did just that, tilted the seat back, and closed my eyes.

"Rise and shine, Sleeping Beauty," Charlie said. I thought I'd dosed off for just a brief moment, but there was the downtown skyline just ahead of us. "You want to be dropped off at home, or some sexy thing's house? Just tell me where."

"Oh, man, sorry about that, I guess I was really out. If it's not too much trouble would it be okay if you dropped me off at my office? I spoke to my office mate this morning, he said he'd be there, and with everything that was going on, well I lost my set of keys."

"That's your pal Louie, right?"

"Yeah, how'd you know?"

"What? Oh you must have mentioned him at some point. Didn't you tell me you were going to call him last night?"

"Probably," I said, pretty sure I didn't mention Louie's name, or anyone else's for that matter.

I gave Charlie directions to my office and we pulled up in front not ten minutes later.

"You want me to wait while you run up there? Just in case your pal's not here."

"Thanks, Charlie, but not necessary. I'm sure he'll be there." I turned to face him and said, "I'm kind of at a loss here. You really looked after me, God, I wouldn't even be here if it hadn't been for you. Tubby's guys were going to kill me."

Charlie nodded. "Yeah, they were, but that's in the past, you need to put it there and then lock it away. Like I said, when it was all said and done, you were the only one who tried to help Daryl. I appreciate that more than you'll ever know. You need anything, Dev, don't hesitate to call."

"Same goes for you, Charlie, you ever need anything just let me know," I said then we shook hands and I climbed out.

Charlie gave me a little wave and pulled away, a moment later, the red Escalade pulled away from the curb up the block and drove past. No one in the vehicle bothered to look at me. I watched the cars until they'd driven out of sight then went in and climbed the stairs to my office.

"Hey, just in time. I got a fresh pot going," Louie said as I came through the door. He was standing in front of his picnic table desk, holding a mug full of steaming coffee. "You enjoy your little vacation? You said you were up North, I want all the disgusting details, who was she?"

I smiled and suddenly felt very tired. "The bad news is, there wasn't anyone. I guess the good news is, I'm here to tell the story."

Louie looked at me for a moment and you could see the wheels turning in his head. Then he shrugged, sat down, and put his feet up on the picnic table. He slurped some coffee, spilling some on his shirt in the process. "God, that's hot," he said and bolted upright.

"Nice to see some things never change," I said then settled in behind my desk.

"You okay?" Louie asked some time later. He'd been going over a couple of files, while I continued to just stare out the window.

"Yeah, just tired is all. Thinking."

"Thinking, hmmm-mmm, that must be why I didn't recognize the look," Louie said. He went back to reviewing his files, then left for a court appointment a little after one. Later that afternoon I phoned Heidi.

"Hi, Heidi."

"Well, mystery guest. Where have you been?"

"I was just up North for a couple of days."

"Really? Doing anything interesting?"

"No."

"Are you okay, Dev?"

"Yeah, I'm fine, not to worry. Just checking in, I guess."

"Why don't you come over tonight? I've got a meeting at five, but it shouldn't last too long. Can you make it for dinner, say seven?"

"Yeah, actually that would be great."

"You sure you're okay? I don't know, it's like you just sound sort of different or something."

"Yeah, I'm fine, thanks for asking. I'll see you tonight, seven. I'll bring a bottle of wine."

"That would be perfect. Call me if anything comes up, otherwise I'll see you tonight, don't be late."

I hung up the phone and stared out the window until it was time to go to Heidi's. I suddenly realized I didn't have a car. I walked four blocks to the liquor store, picked up a couple bottles of wine, then hailed a taxi as it drove past. On the way to Heidi's, I had the driver go past Crickett's house. There was a freshly planted for sale sign in the front yard. I had him pull to the curb and I got out and rang her doorbell. I rang it a couple times, but she never answered.

I peered in the living room window, the room was empty except for four or five boxes stacked in the middle of the floor. There was a folded baby stroller leaning against the boxes. I think the stroller was the one she'd had Oliver in when she ran into me at The Spot a thousand years ago. Apparently Charlie had moved pretty fast.

"You looking to buy a place?" the cabbie asked when I climbed back in.

"Oh, just a wild thought. I wanted to check that place out, but after taking a quick look, it's not right for me." I was at Heidi's door a few minutes later.

"Amazingly, right on time," she said opening the door, then took the bottles of wine from me and we walked back into her kitchen. She was wearing her standard fantastic outfit then oddly, had an apron wrapped around her that was so splattered it made her look like she'd just survived the St. Valentine's Day massacre. "Big surprise, I'm actually cooking this meal, Dev," she said then stepped back and looked at me. "You okay? You seem, I don't know, different."

"Me? Yeah I'm fine."

"You look like you need a lot more than a hug, but let's start there," she said and then wrapped her arms around me and squeezed. "You sure you're okay?" she asked a moment later when she'd stepped back.

"I told you, I'm just fine."

"Okay, if you say so. You just, I don't know, you seem a little different. Anyway, nothing that some home cooking can't fix. I'm making pasta."

She said it like it was some sort of major undertaking. I didn't feel the need to point out you basically just boiled water. Her kitchen sink had three pans, a couple of bowls, various kitchen utensils, and something that looked like a section of rain gutter already stacked in it. The kitchen counter was hidden under a layer of flour and eggshells. Various spice containers and empty food packages were strewn about. There was a foot long slash of what looked like tomato sauce running down the white subway tiles on one of the walls.

"Wow, looks like you've been busy. So, you're cooking, actually cooking, and not just reheating?"

"Shut up and open the wine. I took a lesson if you must know."

"A lesson?" I said, getting the corkscrew out of a drawer.

"Yeah, they handed out about thirty different dinner recipes, plus I'm baking French bread, a baguette in case you're interested."

"Impressive. When did you become Julia Child?"

"Who?"

"Not important. Hey, I'm duly impressed," I said, then handed her a glass and raised mine in a toast.

Chapter Forty-Four

"**Okay admit it, this** just really sucks" Heidi said and stabbed her fork disgustedly into her pasta bowl. "God, I should have just ordered in a pizza. Nothing turned out, did it? Tell me the truth."

"I think you're being just a little hard on yourself. It's a really good first effort." We were eating in the dining room. I wasn't sure we'd ever get the kitchen back to a semblance of normal, and Heidi was right, the food was awful.

She must have thrown the entire pasta package into the pot. There was enough spaghetti to easily feed another ten people. Not that they'd eat any more than we had. Our plates remained largely untouched. She'd burned the baguette, turned the thing to charcoal bits. She was supposed to bake it in the rain gutter thing, but for some reason had laid it on the metal rack, where it dripped through onto the electric coils at the bottom of her oven. That set the smoke alarm off, the first time. It went off again, when she'd burned the pasta sauce while attending to the oven disaster. In an effort to compensate, and balance things out, she'd undercooked the pasta. It didn't crunch, but it was a pretty long way from what you'd call the tender stage. I was wishing I'd gotten four bottles of wine instead of just two.

"God, I just can't do this shit," she said, then held out her empty wine glass and wiggled it from side to side.

"I think it's a pretty good first effort, honest," I said.

"Oh shut up, I've got some Snickers ice cream bars in the freezer, want one?"

"I'd love one, I'll get them," I said, then got out of my chair and picked up our pasta bowls still heaped to overflowing with Heidi's inedible attempt at Italian cuisine.

"Yes, please just get it out of my sight, thank you," she said and refocused her attention on the glass of wine.

I pushed through the swinging door into the kitchen it was an even bigger disaster, than when I'd first arrived. It smelled like a five alarm fire, the vent fan over the stove was still roaring, and the back door remained open in an effort to get all the smoke out of the kitchen. There wasn't a flat surface anywhere that hadn't been littered with cooking debris. And then there were the two muscle bound guys leaning against the counter.

One of them had the lid off the pan with the burnt pasta sauce and was making a disgusting face as he sniffed the contents. "This smells really bad, man."

I'd foolishly left the Walther at my office. I would have tried to make it to the front door, but that would have left Heidi on her own. The guy sniffing the pasta sauce watched me as I glanced to the far side of the granite counter at Heidi's knife rack.

"Oh, please don't think like that. If we'd wanted to nail you, we would have just walked in and shot you at the dining room table with Miss Fantastic Ass out there. Actually, the honor of your presence has been requested by Tubby Gustafson," he said then made a sweeping sort of gesture with his arm in the general direction of the back door.

"Gee thanks, but I've sort of got other plans," I indicated the kitchen and the disaster that surrounded us.

"Yeah, not that it doesn't need it, but this is a special, very personal invitation, and Tubby isn't the sort to keep waiting. He's just out front. I don't think this will take more than a minute of your time, Mr. Haskell."

The guy seated at the kitchen counter got up off the stool. He was at least six-two with tribal tattoos wrapped around his very large biceps. I recognized him as one of the guys who was pushing the giant inflatable balls the other day and helping dead Reggie. "Please," he said nicely enough, but there was no question, one way or another I was going to meet Tubby Gustafson, now.

It turned out Tubby's limo was parked across the street from Heidi's house. As we approached the guy with the tattooed biceps stepped ahead and said, "Please, allow me, Mr. Haskell." Then he held the door open for me and waited until I climbed in before he closed it.

The limo was long, black, and very shiny. When I climbed in, there sat Tubby, lounging in the far corner, holding a chilled stem glass of something. He was dressed in an off-white suit and a starched white shirt with some sort of food stain dripped along the buttons. It looked like some of Heidi's pasta sauce, and my first thought was *'it serves you right.'*

"Please, join me," he smiled and directed me to the seat opposite him as if I had a choice. I sat down and we stared at one another, while Tubby took a couple of loud gulps and examined me over the rim of his glass.

"Life's funny, isn't it, Mr. Haskell."

"Not lately," I said.

"Look, I hope you're not too upset over the unfortunate events of the other day. Just a slight misunderstanding I'm afraid. You know how it is, right?"

"I'm not sure I do, maybe you could just enlighten me."

"Oh you know, in our haste, certain individuals can be prone to make mistakes. That's all it was, just a simple mistake. I hope you understand, and you'll have the good sense to forgive," he said.

"Forgive you? For trying to kill me?"

"Well now, no need to be quite that specific that was just basic business, and perhaps a bit unfortunate. I'll give you that. But, I'm the one who suffered the substantial loss here, and all because of a lack of information on someone's part. Frankly, I just didn't have all the facts at the time."

"All the facts."

"Why yes, your connections, you see in a way, it's really your fault. All you had to do was tell me you were connected to our good friends up North and none of that awfulness would have happened. It would have been a completely different story. We just didn't know, frankly we had no idea. I thought you were just some stupid, bumbling, pain in the ass fool, bent on causing me headaches."

"Your good friends up North? And that would have made a difference?"

Tubby raised his hands palms up, indicating the two of us facing one another in the back of his limo. "Well, here we are, both of us, you and me, talking like a couple of reasonable gentlemen, and," he pulled back a curtain on the side window to give me a view of the street just as a faded powder blue Integra with a pink trunk pulled up and parked in front of Heidi's. Bulldog stepped out from behind the steering wheel, smiled and gave me a nod.

"To tell you the truth, Mr. Haskell, I had no idea you were connected. If only you had mentioned something, anything, all that unpleasantness would have never occurred. I hope you'll accept my sincere apology, and let your friend know I'm very sorry," Tubby said then bowed his head and tried to look contrite.

"My friend?"

"Your friend up North," he said and raised his eyebrows.

I nodded then asked, "Where does Crickett fall into all of this?"

"Crickett?" His eyes moved up to the right of his thick skull, thinking. "Look, you want her? You can have her, she's all yours."

I shook my head. "Just curious, I guess. No, she deserves the two of you, you and your son."

"I wonder if perhaps we couldn't have a gentleman's agreement not to mention that small indiscretion, ever again." His voice quivered, and his face became flushed as he squeezed the stem of his glass and fought to remain in control, then he drained his glass and burped.

"What are you drinking?" I asked.

"Prosecco, could I interest you in a glass?"

"If you had a bottle to spare, I think I could put it to pretty good use."

He reached past me and pulled down what I thought was an arm rest. I immediately felt the cold air rolling out of the small cooler. He reached in, removed a chilled bottle, and handed it to me. "Now, how's that for service?"

"Yeah, thanks. Anything else? I really should be getting back inside."

"Of course, of course," Tubby said, then reached over and opened the door for me. "Say, Haskell, you won't forget to mention our little conversation to your friend, will you? Let him know I'd like to stay on his good side from here on in."

"I'll be sure to tell him, Tubby. Thanks for this," I said holding up the bottle, then I climbed out and crossed the street.

"Here's your keys," Bulldog said stepping forward. He handed the Feline Rescue key ring back to me. "Got it all washed and detailed for you, too." He attempted to smile, but his face was so unused to the exercise, it came off as more of a sneer.

"Nice," I said, then walked back to Heidi's kitchen door. They were gone by the time I reached the corner of the house.

"What were you doing in there?" Heidi asked, she was still sitting at the dining room table.

"Oh, just starting to straighten up the kitchen a little."

"It's kind of a mess isn't it," she said and put on her dejected face.

"There's no 'kind of' about it, but I'll clean up, you cooked after all."

She brightened up at that.

"Listen, why don't you curl up on the couch, there must be something completely worthless you could watch on TV. How about a glass of Prosecco?"

"I wish we had some."

"As a matter of fact, we do. I brought some."

"You did? I don't recall seeing any when you came in."

"You were all involved preparing dinner," I said, not adding *'and almost poisoning both of us.'* "You go on into the living room, I'll bring a glass out to you."

Over the course of the next ninety minutes, I returned Heidi's kitchen to a semblance of order; I scrubbed the pans, loaded and ran the dishwasher, scoured the countertops, put the spices away, tossed out the various empty packages, mopped the floor, wiped down the subway tiles on the wall and then hauled the remainder of her failed attempt at cooking out to the trash. During that process, I also filled her Prosecco glass five separate times.

When I finally exited the kitchen, she was curled up under a leopard skin fleece, snoring. So much for my good intentions. I left her a note thanking her for dinner, then turned off the light, and locked the door behind me.

I climbed into the Integra. There was a naked lady air freshener hanging in the hole where the radio used to be. A .45 slug rested in the ashtray, compliments of Bulldog, no doubt. I debated for half a second about going back into Heidi's, then fired up the Integra. It was probably just as well, I had a busy day ahead of me.

Chapter Forty-Five

I was up before my alarm went off and heading North. I drove through Vaxholm and out the county road for a mile then turned on the road that led to Charlie's place. The red Escalade was parked in front of the garage. There were a couple of high-powered pickup trucks pulled further ahead. I parked the Integra and climbed out, it continued to sputter and shake as I looked over the roof at two guys sitting on the front porch. They seemed to be enjoying the show.

"You might want to get that looked at," one of them called. His partner chuckled.

I began to make my way up the steps.

"Maybe just hold it right there. What do you want?"

"I'd like to speak to Charlie."

"He's pretty busy right now."

"I'd still like to talk to him, tell him it's Dev Haskell."

The heavier of the two looked annoyed, but pulled himself out of the rocker and walked into the house. I stood there and waited. I noticed a pickup had rolled across the entrance off the road, blocking any exit.

A few minutes later the door opened, and Charlie stepped out. He was holding little Oliver on his hip as he walked to the edge of the porch, and stood there looking down on me. "Dev, I wish you would have called first. I'm a little busy right now."

"Another timely get together, just to make sure everyone is on the same page?"

Charlie smiled. "Yeah, something like that."

"Can we talk, I've got a message from Tubby."

Charlie shook his head, like he was resigned to his fate and would have to endure a conversation with me. He climbed down the steps, "Come on, we'll walk this way," he said and headed toward the garage.

"So he talked to you. I told that bastard he better apologize."

"You told him? Charlie what the hell is going on?"

"It's pretty simple, actually. Just business. Tubby's organization has been, what? Decimated I guess you could say. Unless he has protection, he won't last a week. It just seemed to be in everyone's best interest if Tubby merged."

"You're protecting that fat piece of shit?"

"For the moment."

"But, what about Daryl? And what's with all of this?" I said, sort of pointing in all directions. "Who are these guys? You're into this kind of action?"

"I told you before I'm an entrepreneur," he said, and then switched Oliver to his other arm. "As for Daryl, he made some mistakes and then tried to over compensate. He ended up trying to play the hero in what was actually an even bigger mistake. I'll deal with that in time. For right now, I think all you need to know is that you're safe. Tubby wouldn't dare touch a hair on your head."

I stood there looking confused.

"Sorry you had to drive all this way for nothing. Now, if you'll excuse us, I've got to get back to work. Come on, I'll walk you to your car," he said then headed in that direction.

He held the driver's door for me and watched as I climbed in behind the wheel. As I buckled up, he leaned in and said, "Dev, you're always welcome here, but maybe next time call ahead. Okay?" He nodded, stepped back then gave a wave to the pickup blocking the road and it slowly rolled back as I headed out the drive.

Chapter Forty-Six

Over the course of the next few weeks things seemed to drift back to a semblance of normal. Brenda had called, and bitched me out for calling the cops on her friend, Arturo. Turns out he wasn't there to harm me after all. He was just some friend with benefits who had a key to her place, and had dropped in for a walk on the wild side. She had remained passed out while the cops hauled him off to jail. I could hear her cats meowing in the background when she called, and my arms immediately began to itch.

I never did run into Crickett. I don't even know if she's still in the state. I wouldn't be if I were her. I did hear Tubby's kid, Ben was shipped out to California for an 'internship'. One can only imagine. Maybe Crickett landed out there and is okay, too, maybe.

Heidi vowed not to take any more cooking classes. It's the small things that make life worth living.

The End

Thanks for taking the time to read <u>Crickett</u>. If you enjoyed the read please tell 2-300 of your closest friends. Don't miss the sample of <u>Bulldog</u> that follows my shameless self promotion.

Help yourself to my other titles. They're all available on Amazon.

The following are all stand alone titles;

Baby Grand

Chow For Now

Slow, Slow, Quick, Quick

Merlot

Finders Keepers

End of the Line

Irish Dukes (Fight Card Series) written under the pseudonym Jack Tunney

The following titles comprise the Dev Haskell series;
Russian Roulette: (1)
Mr. Swirlee: (2)
Bite Me: (3)
Bombshell: (4)
Tutti Frutti: (5)
Last Shot: (6)
Ting-A-Ling: (7)
Cricket: (8)
Bulldog: (9)
Double Trouble (10)
Twinkle Toes:
(A Dev Haskell short story)

Email: mikefaricyauthor@gmail.com
Facebook: Mike Faricy Books
Facebook: Dev Haskell
Twitter: @mikefaricybooks

Here's a little taste of <u>Bulldog</u>, the ninth in the Dev Haskell series, enjoy.

Bulldog
Mike Faricy

Chapter One

The first time I saw Dermot Gallagher his right hand held a pint of Mankato Ale and his left arm automatically wrapped around shapely, sexy Casey, the girl who'd come to the bar with me. We were best friends by the end of the night, Dermot and me. Me and Casey...well not so much.

Dermot had been in his uniform that night, a black tunic and a saffron kilt. He was a drummer in an Irish bagpipe band here in town. Maybe that was it, the uniform or maybe Casey just had a thing for guys in skirts, I don't know. He turned out to be a really good guy, with a dry sense of humor, sort of quiet, but only because he was taking note of everything going on around him. He had dark hair, wore glasses and stood about six feet tall with a ready smile. He and Casey were married the following year. I was deployed at the time.

The smile was gone today. The mortician did a pretty decent job, but if you knew Dermot like I did, well it just wasn't the same. The white silk lining on the inside of his casket didn't do much to help matters.

There was a rosary wrapped around his hands. I never knew him to be particularly religious, hell maybe he wasn't and he was just hedging his bets. That would be just like him, a final, subtle joke on his way out the door. We'd lost guys when I was deployed, even so you never get used to it and that experience certainly didn't make this any easier.

"You about ready, Dev? I guess they're lining up at the door to carry him in," Casey placed a hand on my arm and gently pulled me away from Dermot. It was a few minutes before eleven. The visitation in the vestibule of the church had been going on for a couple of hours and the place was packed.

Casey was a little thing, maybe five-two, blue eyed with a slight figure. She was dressed in black and proving herself a hell of a lot stronger than me right now. I walked over to where the priest and the other pall bearers were assembled and waited quietly.

The undertaker rolled Dermot's wooden coffin up to the doors going into the chapel then directed us in a soft voice. "Line up here, lads, three to a side. We'll raise him up then arms on the shoulder of the man across from you. No rush, we'll walk at a modest pace to the front and you'll set him on the stand before the altar. All right now, everyone ready?"

A couple of guys nodded, I guess I was still too numb. We took hold of the brass handles and hoisted the coffin up to shoulder height, rested it on our arms stretched to the man's shoulder across from us, then after a nod from the undertaker we stepped off. At least three of us had been in the service which put everyone more or less in step. Not that Dermot was particularly heavy, it was just I don't know, I can't remember really. I was okay for the first few steps, then the organ started playing and I came close to losing it. A clearing of the throat and a hard swallow got me back in line. We carried him up the aisle, then back out at the end of the service an hour later.

I don't remember much, Casey and her extended family walked behind us on the way out. She carried a large, framed photograph of Dermot giving everyone a last look, tears were running down her cheeks and she was biting her lip, but she made it.

We carried Dermot to the hearse and after the short drive to the cemetery, from the hearse to the grave site. Dermot's band was there, twenty some folks standing in formation playing Amazing Grace on the bagpipes while we carried him to his final resting place. God, and I thought the church had been tough. The moment I heard that tune tears started running down *my* cheeks.

And then it was over.

Chapter Two

We were back at The Spot for a farewell toast and a bite to eat. It was crowded and there was a lot of false bravado being shouted back and forth. Casey was holding a Jameson with a brother on either side for support. She came from a tight family and they would make sure she was okay. Folks kept coming up to give her a hug and pay their respects. I don't think she ever got the chance to take a first sip.

"Get you a beer?"

I turned around to see my pal, Aaron LaZelle a lieutenant in St. Paul's homicide department. Detective Norris Manning was behind him and gave me a polite nod.

"Thanks, but no thanks. If I start today I may not stop."

"You gonna be okay?" He sounded like he really meant it. Manning had turned away and was eyeing the assembled crowd.

"Yeah, I'm fine this is just a tough one."

"They're all senseless, but this one, Jesus," Aaron said and shook his head.

"Any idea, any leads."

He shook his head again, then said, "Nothing of any consequence at this point, but we're not about to give up."

Of course what else could he say? "You need anything from me you just give the word," I said.

"Actually, what we need is you not getting involved. I know how you feel, believe me we've both been there." Manning turned and nodded agreement then went back to scanning the crowd.

I saw no point in commenting.

"You let us do our job and we'll get whoever did this, Dev. I promise."

"Just for the record, the guy had no enemies. He wouldn't hurt a fly, same with his wife, Casey. They're just good folks."

It was Aaron's turn to nod. "That's what we heard over and over, just the nicest folks."

"Still the same story?" I asked. "He just answered the door and some bastard shot him?"

"It seems to look that way at this point. I'd say the wife's scream from upstairs frightened off whoever was there. It's just not making a lot of sense at this stage, but then does it ever? Like I said, we'll get whoever is responsible."

I was going to say something like '*I hope you get them before I do,*' but a little voice inside my head said '*Shut up, stupid,*' and for once, I listened. Looking back, I think that was probably the first inkling that I wasn't going to wait. If I'm yelling, my temper might be on the loose for a moment, but I quickly get it back in check. It's when I'm quiet or soft-spoken that I'm probably the most dangerous. I can become cold, very unforgiving, and I'm capable of some horrible things. I'd been that way from the moment I learned someone murdered my friend, Dermot.

"Anyone seem out of place here?" Aaron asked. Manning was still scanning the crowd.

I shook my head. "Most of these folks I know. Like I said, everyone loved the guy. It just doesn't make any sense and I'm not buying the random option."

"It's possible, but the chances of it ever being random are pretty slight. There's always the off chance some loon is in the crowd here getting high on people's reactions or the sense of tragedy. You know, suddenly they think they're important because they caused all this," Aaron said.

"Jesus."

"Yeah. Well, I think we'll be going. I'm not going to pay my respects. It's always a bit disingenuous and just seems to add more stress to an already stressful situation."

I nodded then said, "I meant it. You need anything on this you let me know."

"We'll do that, Dev. You let us handle it. I know it doesn't seem like we're moving fast enough, but give us some time, promise?"

"Yeah, sure."

"Counting on you, Dev," Aaron said then he and Manning sort of faded into the crowd and out the door.

"Was that the police you were talking to earlier?" Casey asked maybe an hour later. The crowd had begun to thin out, but I still didn't think she'd ever had the chance to sip her drink. She'd set the thing down a while ago and apparently lost track of it.

"Yeah, I've known the one guy, the lieutenant since we were kids. The other guy is a detective, I've dealt with him in the past." I saw no point in mentioning Manning had me fingered as the root of all crime, major and not so major, committed in the city.

"What did they want?"

"Just checking on things, they like to make sure everything is as good as can be expected for you," I lied.

"Oh, that's kind of sweet."

"Yeah, that's them."

"Hey, my brother's and some friends are coming back to the house after this, it would be nice if you could join us," she said.

"Thanks."

"No pressure, it's going to be laid back. Hope you can make it." She turned around when a woman tapped her on the shoulder to express her regrets and say how truly sorry she was. Poor Casey was on about hour six of listening to the same well-intentioned comments, which in itself would be exhausting.

Chapter Three

"**No, she seems pretty** set on selling the place,"
Dennis said. He was one of Casey's brothers. Another
brother, Tommy was reaching into the refrigerator and
passing beers our way. We were in Casey's kitchen,
nibbling from a dozen different plates of hors
d'oeuvres.

"God, they just got the place," I said.

"Well yeah, more like two years now, but what a
mess, it's almost a hundred and twenty-five-years old
and right now there isn't a room that's not torn up. God
bless the two of them, but finishing a project wasn't
their strong suit. Jesus, talk about stars in your eyes,"
Tommy said, then gave a quick glance around the
room.

There wasn't a door hung on any of the kitchen
cabinets. Sections of plywood painted black had served
as the temporary counter tops for the past year. One of
the exterior walls had been opened up and yellow
fiberglass insulation was wedged between the studs and
covered with a plastic vapor barrier. The ceiling had
been gutted down to the joists and you could see the
cloth covered copper wire from about 1915 running
through holes in the true dimension timber. Next to the

wires, the pipe from the 1890 gas light ran to the middle of the room.

"We got some guys coming in to hang some sheetrock and do taping, we hope to be painting after that."

"What about an electrician and a plumber, is this joint even up to code?" I asked.

"They're starting Monday, sheetrockers will have to work around them, but we need to get this place on the market. We wait much longer and we might as well wait until next spring. Christ, not much moves in real estate between November and March in Minnesota."

"Is she gonna stay here, I mean while the work is being done?" I asked.

Tommy shook his head. "My two girls are down in Madison at college, we got extra space. She can be as private as she wants or needs to be, she's staying with us until she gets resettled, there's no rush. She was just uncomfortable staying here, no surprise, so she's been with us the last couple of nights."

"How's she doing?"

"Like anyone would, I guess. She's in the bedroom a lot of the time. Comes out and you can tell she's been crying, her eyes are red and puffy, she's sniffling. What can you do except give her a big hug and tell her you love her. Of course then that just starts her up again. I can hear her up in the middle of the night walking the floor. It's gonna take some time."

"So, Casey mentioned you're a PI?" Dennis said then took a sip from his beer and shot a quick glance toward his brother.

"Yeah, I am, but I mostly work on stuff like resumes to employers and things. You know, just making sure job applications are correct and some dork hasn't listed himself as the president of a bank when in fact he's out there delivering newspapers or something."

"So you wouldn't investigate something like this, Dermot's murder?"

"No," I said then took a deep breath in preparation to give the company line. "In an investigation like this, the best thing, the most helpful thing we can all do, is stay out of the way. Give any and all information, even the most remote, seemingly unimportant fact, just give it to the cops. They're equipped to deal with these things. They'll process DNA samples, ask questions, interview folks. They don't need any of us out there screwing things up, and they especially don't need me making a mess of their investigation."

"Sounds like you've already backed off without even taking a look," Dennis said.

"Denny, come on, man," Tommy said.

"No, it's okay, he's right, that is what it sounds like, but I do this for a living, and I have for some time. I know for a fact whatever I do, won't help. Whatever any of us do, unless it's passing on information, is just going to muddy the water and at best slow down the job the cops have to do. At worst it could quite possibly screw things up to the point where they don't catch the bastard. I don't want that on my conscience. I want to see whoever is responsible get nailed."

"You any good at taping sheetrock?" Dennis asked changing the subject.

"No, but I can paint ceilings and walls. You get that sheetrock up, you call me and I'll help you get this place on the market."

"Deal, you need another beer?" Tommy said and opened the refrigerator.

"No thanks, fellas, I got some things I have to get accomplished today. I better find Casey and say my goodbyes. Here," I said and pulled a business card out of my wallet. "Give me a call and I'll help you paint this place."

"Thanks, we'll do that. Nice to meet you, Dev," Tommy said.

"Thanks," Dennis called as I headed for the front of the house.

"You dipshit, what did you say that shit for?" Tommy said as I left the room. I walked beyond earshot and never heard the reply.

Chapter Four

It was a couple of nights later. I was in The Spot sitting with Louie talking about everything and nothing. I share an office with Louie, and he pretends to be my attorney from time to time. Actually he's a pretty good guy and has gotten me out of more than a couple of jams. It was obvious, and I appreciated the fact, that Louie had steered away from any mention of Dermot or Casey Gallagher.

"Mike, maybe just one more round," Louie said, then waved his index finger in a sort of circle to signal the same again.

"You clowns said that about two hours ago, and you're still here."

"Lucky you," Louie said.

My phone rang. I could only hope it was Heidi in need of some of my *special* attention.

"Haskell Investigations."

"Dev?"

"You got me."

"Dev, it's Casey. Hey, sorry to bother you, but I'm at the house packing some things up and this car has been going around the block, slowing down in front of the house, then going through the alley checking the back of the house. It's really freaking me out."

"Did you call the cops, call 911?"

"Yeah, but they didn't seem too impressed. They said they'd send a squad car over, but it wasn't a high priority. Something about concert traffic downtown and stuff. It's just really freakin' me out and, oh shit, there he is again. It's this sinister looking black thing, I don't know maybe I'm just losing it. No answer at either one of my brothers so I'm calling you."

"You just stay there, make sure your doors are locked and stay away from the windows. Okay?"

"Oh God, I'm sorry to be such a pain."

"It's not a problem, we're on our way. You just stay put we're maybe five minutes out."

"Thanks, Dev."

I hung up the phone and said, "Come on, I gotta go to Casey's"

"I just ordered a round," Louie said.

"Mike, hang onto those drinks, we'll be back for them," I said then pulled Louie off his stool and out the door. My Saturn was parked almost in front. "Get in the back seat," I called to Louie as I hurried around the side.

"What?"

"That passenger side door isn't fixed yet so it's tied shut."

"Tied shut?"

"Just get in," I said and slid behind the wheel. The starter groaned and cranked for a long moment then fired up just as Louie got in. I pulled away from the curb before he had the door closed.

"Jesus Christ, what is this, NASCAR?"

"Better buckle up," I said and floored the thing down Victoria heading for 35E.

"You're gonna get stopped," Louie said from the back seat and I heard his seat belt click.

"They try and stop me, they can just follow me to Casey's, too busy with a concert to see what's going on, God."

We made it to the 35E entrance in record time, the entrance ramp is up a slight incline and the speed limit on this section of interstate through town is posted at just forty-five miles per hour. I screeched around the corner onto the entrance ramp then accelerated, we were doing sixty-five and climbing as we shot onto the interstate.

"Dev, come on, another two minutes isn't going to make a difference."

"Hey, some jack-off shot Dermot last week when he opened the door. No one has done a damn thing about it except say how unfortunate it was. Now someone's circling the place and the cops can't be bothered because there's too many folks trying to get to a concert or some bullshit. I'll take my chances speeding, but you better hope whoever is freaking her out has left by the time we get there."

We took the Grand Ave exit off the interstate. The light was red where the exit runs into Ramsey. I slowed just enough to check for oncoming traffic, then ran the light with a left hand turn and stomped on the accelerator heading up Ramsey Hill.

Louie had enough sense not to say anything.

Casey and Dermot's home was on Holly Ave. It's a quiet residential street of Victorian homes built close together. The street is edged with granite curb stones and narrow enough that parking is allowed on only one side. I zipped around the corner onto Holly, then pulled to a stop in front of Casey's place a few seconds later. I grabbed the .38 snub out of the glove compartment. It only held five rounds, but it was all I had at the moment.

I was halfway to the front door, just about to take the front steps two at a time before Louie even opened the car door. There was a picture window in the front of the house with a building permit taped to the glass. A stained glass window in a grape leaf design sat above that. I rang the doorbell then remembered it didn't work and pounded on the door. It looked like Casey had turned on every light in the house. A high pitched voice answered from behind the door a moment later. "Who is it?"

"Casey, it's Dev, open up."

A lock snapped, the heavy door swung open and Casey stood there wide-eyed. "Oh God, I'm glad to see you. Thanks for coming," she said then saw the .38 in my hand and her eyes grew wider. "Did you shoot him?"

"I haven't seen anyone yet," I said.

She looked past my shoulder and suddenly gave a long, "Oh..."

I turned to see Louie waddling up the front sidewalk. "It's okay, he's with me. Casey, this is Louie Laufen, Louie, Casey Gallagher."

"Hi," Casey sort of mumbled.

"Nice to meet ya," Louie said sounding out of breath.

"Louie, wait inside with Casey. I'm going to walk around the house, then maybe do a quick drive around the block. Have you seen anyone since we talked?"

Casey shook her head no.

Louie groaned his way up the four front steps. The porch floor creaked with his weight as he walked past me toward Casey and the front door.

"I'll see you two in a couple of minutes," I said and made my way around the back of the house.

I had no idea what I was looking for and there was at least a fifty-fifty chance there wasn't anything *to* look for. Maybe it was just someone looking for an address or a neighbor out for a short drive. Casey had recently been through a traumatic experience and it wasn't that far fetched to say she could be imagining things.

Her garage was locked. All the first floor windows on the house seemed to be secure, the back door was locked. The gate leading out to the alley was closed, an expensive gas grill was still on the deck and the umbrella was still in the glass-topped picnic table. Things appeared to be pretty much in order.

Chapter Five

"I'm sorry I acted like such a baby," Casey said.

Louie and I were sipping Jameson in her den. Casey was nursing a cup of chamomile tea. The room had ten-foot ceilings and wide molding painted white around the windows and sliding panel doors. The fire place had a white marble mantel with a large gilt mirror on the wall above it. Green-glazed Victorian fireplace tiles rested in three cardboard boxes on the granite hearth. Casey caught me staring at the tiles.

"They were loose and some had fallen off so we pulled them all off when we had the chimney relined. We were going to reset them this winter, or maybe the next," she said absently.

"Describe this car to me that was driving around," I said.

"Well, I saw it out the upstairs window. I'm bringing more clothes back to Tommy's, so I was upstairs in the master bedroom packing them," she said then nodded toward a half dozen boxes stacked near the front door. "At first I didn't pay any attention, but then probably the third time I saw it drive by it frightened me. It's was dark blue or black, probably black, kinda low slung like and it's all black, even the wheels and the rims. It was evil looking and like I said, it just freaked me out."

"And it slowed down in front of your house?" I asked.

"Yeah, more than slowed down it almost came to a complete stop like it was looking for something, I don't know maybe checking out our address. Then it would go around the block. I don't know why, but after a bunch of times I went into the back bedroom upstairs. I left the light off and a moment later there he was doing the same thing at the back of the house, just sort of sat there looking at the place, then it slowly drove off. Maybe five minutes later the thing was back out there in front of the house." She nodded out toward the street. "Whoever it was, they were definitely checking this place out. That's when I went around and turned on all the lights. I wanted them to think this place was really crowded like we were having a party or something."

"You're thinking of selling this, right?" I asked.

"There's no thinking about it. I just want to be rid of it. I can't stand to…" her voice trailed off and she sat there with her eyes tearing up biting her lip and trying not to cry.

I waited a long moment before I spoke.

"Maybe it was someone who heard you were going to put this on the market and was just driving past to check it out."

"Maybe, but I haven't even talked with a realtor yet."

That slimmed down the possibility, but I said, "Yeah, but I knew and maybe a couple other folks. Could be one of your brothers mentioned it and someone was just taking a look."

"Could be it was someone who was just curious," Louie said. "I think the address was in the news, you know, after...."

"It just really made me feel uncomfortable. What if they come back when I'm not here and do something like burn the place down? After what's happened, I mean they could do anything, right?"

"I think that's highly unlikely," Louie said.

"After what's already happened, this town is full of crazies. God, that's all I need is some idiot burning the house down. I just can't seem to catch a break."

"Tell you what, how about if we help you load that stuff in the car," I nodded toward the boxes stacked by the front door. "Then you give Louie a ride back to his car and if it will make you feel any better, I'll stay here."

"Oh, you don't have to do that, Dev." But she said it in a way that wasn't leaving me very much wiggle room.

"Not a problem, it would be my pleasure."

"You sure? I mean, maybe I'm just being neurotic or something."

"No, in fact the more I think about it, the more it sounds like a good idea. I want to do it, please."

"You're sure?" she said and sort of shrugged her shoulders

"Yeah, I insist, come on, let's get you loaded up."

"Okay," and suddenly Casey was on her feet and all smiles.

Damn it.

Chapter Six

On her way out the door Casey had told me to help myself to anything I could find. I was on my second beer with a bowl of chicken wings and some sort of dip and fancy crackers left over from Dermot's funeral. I had everything spread out on the coffee table. The Big Lebowski was playing on the flat screen and I was stretched out on the leather couch. The movie was just at the point where the Dude was in the bath tub smoking a joint while listening to whale sounds, when I heard something toward the back of the house.

Once Casey and Louie finally left I'd gone through the house and turned off most of the lights. I was flaked out on the couch in the den where I planned to sleep and just had a table lamp on for light. I heard the noise again, put the movie on pause, grabbed the .38 and walked out of the den, through the dining room and into the kitchen. There was a small room off the back of the kitchen that served as the laundry room, but the back door was actually off a small porch on the side of the kitchen.

I stood there in the dark leaning against the kitchen sink waiting and looking at the wall across the room. I moved my eyes back and forth between two windows across from where I stood. The windows were maybe six feet apart and about five feet tall. From the outside of the house a person could stand on the little porch where the windows were and really not be seen.

I heard the noise at almost the same time I saw the shadowy figure. The individual was kind of tall and looked fairly broad. I slowly approached holding the .38 out in front of me in a two-handed grip with the thing aimed at his head.

As I moved closer, the face came into focus and I actually recognized the idiot. The flattened nose, the Mohawk hairstyle, a half dozen piercings in each eyebrow and the three rings in his bottom lip left little doubt. Then, there was the gauging in his earlobes the size of a giant doughnut hole. I didn't so much know him as I knew of him. Freddy Zimmerman, Fat Freddy, a wannabe criminal of dubious reputation. I was pretty sure he was a general disappointment to folks on both sides of the law.

Last I heard, Freddy had been trying to win favor with local crime boss Tubby Gustafson by following Tubby around in an attempt to offer 'additional protection'. That sort of went down the drain when Freddy rear ended Tubby's Mercedes at a stoplight and Tubby's morally impaired enforcer, a jerk named Bulldog, jumped out of the vehicle and made the adjustments that resulted in Freddy's dinner plate nose. I was tempted to shoot, but it would be a waste of a bullet, and then there was the outside chance it would just bounce off his thick skull anyway.

Instead, I flicked on the porch light and watched as Freddy jumped then dropped whatever tool he was using in his worthless attempt to force the window open. He waddled off the back porch and out into the alley toward his car. The 'sinister' looking black Chevy Camaro Casey had described.

Freddy had cleverly left the car almost directly under the alley light. It appeared to be running with the headlights still on. I watched as he beat his hasty retreat out the back gate, past the trash bins and into the alley.

I walked out the front door, climbed into my Saturn and prayed it would start. I drove up the block and rounded the corner as Fat Freddy peeled out of the alley and took off. I followed Freddy at a distance although I had a pretty good idea where he was headed. Along the way I wondered where a numbskull like Freddy got the sort of cash it would take to purchase that Camaro, provided it was indeed purchased and not 'obtained'.

Sure enough, about five minutes later, he pulled into the parking lot of a dive bar named Ozzie's. I waited about thirty seconds and pulled in after him. I sat in the Saturn for a few minutes then went in the back door and spotted him alone at the bar. It wasn't that surprising, who'd want to spend time with Freddy? He was a moron and besides, there were just two other drinkers in the place. They were nursing beers, appeared to be regulars and didn't look up when I walked in giving the distinct impression they would like to just be left alone.

Freddy looked like his usual idiot self. He glanced in my direction and then attempted to hide his face as I came through the back door. His back was to me and he seemed to be studying the front door, maybe calculating if he could waddle out that way and make it to his Camaro before I caught up with him.

The bartender slid a bottle of beer in front of him and then stood there waiting for payment. Eventually he raised both hands, palms up and sort of wiggled his fingers in a *'Come on, man, pay up'* motion.

"I'll get it, and give me a pint of Mankato Ale," I said then tossed a ten on the bar. The bartender grabbed the ten and nodded, then gave Freddy a strange look. He was back with my beer a minute later. I tossed a five on the bar and he looked at me. "Keep it, I'd like to be private with this gentleman for a moment."

"Suit yourself," he said sounding like I'd made a really bad choice, then rapped the bar a couple of times with his knuckles to acknowledge the tip before he moved to the far end.

Freddy grabbed his beer and took a healthy sip keeping his back to me.

I stuck my little finger in his ear gauge and pulled.

"Ouch, hey what the...God you're killing me, stop it, stop it, dude. Christ, you're gonna rip my ear, bitch."

"Then look at me, Freddy. Where the hell are your manners? How have you been?" I said and pulled my finger out of his ear. His voice had a nasally tone which I guessed came from the nose adjustment Bulldog had given him after rear ending Tubby Gustafson's Mercedes.

"Oh, it's you," he said rubbing his ear lobe and shaking his head. "You're that dick guy, right?"

"Private Investigator," I corrected.

"Yeah, that's what I meant, man. Ahhh, thanks for the beer."

"Not a problem, Freddy. So tell me, what have you been up to?"

"Up to? Me? Nothing really."

"Gee, that's funny. See, I was just taking it easy over at a friend's house and all of sudden I hear a noise. Guess what?"

Freddy looked nervous, reached for the beer bottle and drained about half the thing.

"Come on, Freddy, take a guess."

"I ain't got any idea, Mr. Hassle, honest."

"It's Haskell, fuckwit. So, guess who I saw trying to get into my friend's house? Guess who was trying to break in?"

"Oh, I wasn't trying to break in. He just wanted me to see if there was a way to get in there, that's all. I...." All of a sudden he shut up as if it dawned on him he'd already said too much.

"Trying to find a way in? Into *my* friend's house? For who?" I asked then pulled the .38 out of my pocket and shoved it in my waistband making sure Freddy could see my every move.

"I probably shouldn't have said that. I didn't really mean it," he said, sounding even more nervous.

"Hmmm-mmm, does that mean *you* were going to break into *my* friend's house?"

"No, no honest."

"That's good. I didn't think you'd do that, Freddy. At least I hope you wouldn't, because that would make me very mad and I'm sure neither one of us would want that, would we?"

"No, you're right, that wouldn't be good."

"Yeah, right, so who were you checking things out for? Who's trying to get into *my* friend's house?"

"I really can't say."

"Yeah you can, Freddy. You can tell me, after all we're pals. Look, I even bought you a beer."

"Yeah, I know, I already said thanks and all, but I really can't tell you."

"Sure you can, Freddy, well unless you want to see that fancy car of yours out there in the lot maybe get torched and then after I set it on fire, I'm gonna come back in here and look for you."

"Me?"

"Yeah, and I won't be happy, because you're playing me for a sucker and that makes me mad, Freddy. It really does."

"I'm not playing you for a sucker, Mr. Haskell, honest. It's just that he can be kind of mean and all and..."

I stuck my little finger back into Freddy's ear gauge and pulled.

"Ahhh-hhhh, God don't, come on that really hurts. Don't ahhh-hhhh."

"You got about three seconds to tell me, Freddy, or I'm going to rip this thing right out of your ear."

For just a brief moment the bartender looked over from where he was sitting at the far end of the bar watching the ball game, then he went back to watching the TV.

"Three, two..."

"I can't, I can't tell you they'll..."

"One," I half yelled and yanked the gauge out of Freddy's ear.

"Ahhh-hhhh," he screamed loud enough that one of the regulars looked down our way and the bartender stood up off his stool and said, "Take it outside, fellas," in a loud voice.

I grabbed Freddy by the back of the neck and moved him toward the front door.

Freddy had a bloodied hand over his ear and was screaming, "You maniac, are you fucking crazy? God, you tore my damn ear off, what in the hell is wrong with you? Jesus, that hurts."

"Listen to me, you fat assed idiot, I'm gonna tear that gauge off your other ear, give you a matching pair unless you tell me what you were doing trying to get into that house tonight. You think I'm fooling? So help me God you better start talking or I will tear you apart."

"I already told you, I can't, he'll kill me."

"That's exactly what I plan on doing," I said and reached for his other ear.

Freddy pushed me away and started to run for his car. I sort of half jogged and caught up then dropped a foot or two behind while he kept waddling, trying to fish his keys out to unlock the car door. The lights on his Camaro blinked a moment later as he scurried toward the driver's door. He pulled the door open and just as his fat ass was halfway in the car I slammed into the door full force.

It banged against Freddy and he gave a high-pitched yelp then staggered back a step or two. There was a vertical crease along the outside of the door where I slammed into it. I grabbed him by his Mohawk and bounced his head against the doorframe a couple of times. He stumbled back and started to slide down the side of the car. I lifted him with an uppercut to the chin and heard his teeth clack, then drilled him in what was left of his nose.

"Okay, okay, stop it, God. It was Bulldog, Tubby's guy. Okay, you happy? Jesus, lay off, bitch, I didn't do anything to you. God!"

"Bulldog?"

Freddy was bending over at the waist leaning against the Camaro with his hands on his knees. Blood from his nose and mouth was dripping down into a puddle on the asphalt parking lot. Blood from his ear had soaked a good portion of his shoulder and the front of his shirt. He stared at the ground and didn't look up at me when he spoke.

"Yeah, Bulldog. He didn't tell me why, honest he didn't. He just said he wanted to get into the house, that the folks were moving and he was thinking of buying it back. Wanted to see what they'd done before he came up with a number."

"Buy it back?"

"Yeah, that's what he said, honest," Freddy gasped.

"Why didn't he just call? That doesn't make any sense," I half said to myself, but Freddy heard me.

"I don't know, man. It's Bulldog, it's not supposed to make sense. He just told me to go there and find a way in. He said no one was living there. If I knew your friend was there I wouldn't have tried the window, really, I wouldn't lie to you. I promise I wouldn't," Freddy said then coughed and spit more blood a couple of times onto the asphalt.

...Thanks for taking the time, things are bound to get a little dicey for Dev and he doesn't exactly seem to be in a jovial mood. Better grab a copy of Bulldog and check him out.

Mike Faricy